Praise for the **Loon Lake Mysteries Series**

"[Victoria Houston] puts me right there in the Wisconsin heat and cold, lets me know what the fish are biting on, lets me spy on the interesting characters of Loon Lake, and, most of all, spins an intelligent and captivating tale. I look forward to more and more."
—**T. Jefferson Parker,** author of *Silent Joe*

"Victoria Houston's ... plots and clues invariably involve fly and bait fishing. The formula works: Houston is the best-selling author down at Madison's Booked For Murder mystery bookstore."
—*Chicago Tribune*

"A likable change of pace from some of the more grisly whodunits populating the best-seller lists. Houston populates her little burg with two engaging protagonists and a steady stream of mildly eccentric townies as she leisurely moves a clever plot toward a suspenseful and satisfying conclusion."
—*Booklist*

"What a great story! A book that fishermen of all ages (and species) are sure to enjoy."   —**Tony Rizzo,** author of *Secrets of a Muskie Guide*

"Houston introduces us to a cast of characters with whom we quickly bond—as fly-fishers and as good citizens—in the first of what I hope will be a long series."—**Joan Wulff,** world-class fly-caster, co-founder of the Wulff School of Fly-Fishing

"A compelling thriller—populated with three-dimensional characters who reveal some of their secrets of trout fishing the dark waters of the northern forests."   —**Tom Wiench,** dedicated fly-fisherman and member of Trout Unlimited

# Dead Renegade

# Dead Renegade

## victoria houston

 A LOON LAKE MYSTERY

Published by Bleak House Books
A Big Earth Publishing company
1637 Pearl Street, Suite 201
Boulder, CO 80302
www.bigearthpublishing.com

Printed in the United States of America
14   13   12   11   10      1   2   3   4   5   6   7

Library of Congress data on file

978-1-60648-061-8 (hardcover)
978-1-60948-062-5 (paperback)
978-1-60648-063-2 (Evidence Collection)

*For that man in the boat: Mike*

*Those to whom evil is done,*

*Do evil in return.*

——W. H. Auden

CHAPTER 1

Osborne paused, surprised to see a fan of tail feathers stick-
ing out from one end of an old rug that had been rolled up
and crammed into a dank corner of the storeroom. Not that it
wasn't a welcome sight—a brief respite from the frustrations of
the morning. If he checked that out, he could feel satisfied that
he had indeed searched every inch of the space assigned to him.

Anxious to get a closer look at the feathers, he squeezed
sideways between two beat-up desks festooned with enough
rusted metal strips to cause him to consider the timing of his last
tetanus shot. Lockjaw was the least of his worries, however. He
was not going to get himself and the ladies safely out of here unless he could find some way to smooth over what had escalated
into a touchy situation between two people, each accusing the
other of lying, and, wouldn't you know, one of them a lawyer. A
lawyer who happened to be his own daughter.

Avoiding the issue was not the answer and he knew it. He
just wished it hadn't come to this: minutes ticking away as they
neared the end of what now appeared to have been a fruitless
search. What if neither he, nor Erin, nor her client, were able to
find what they came for? What does he say then?

Does he flat out accuse Bart Nystrom of attempting to rob the elderly widow? Whether or not that is the case, Bart's response would not be pleasant. Could involve accusations of slander, trespassing, ruining a reputation, indulging a crazy old lady, etc. And all sure to be expressed in profane language. Heck of a start to a sunny Thursday in late June. On the other hand, he could offer Bart an easy out.

Not that he deserved it. Osborne wasn't the only Loon Lake resident well aware that Bart, who had inherited the family business, was also heir to endearing (or is it *enduring?*) Nystrom traditions. Traditions such as selling reproductions of Scandinavian furniture as original antiques, exaggerating the size and weight of fish he caught, rolling back the odometer before selling his car—and taking advantage of little old ladies.

This, in addition to Osborne's personal experience with Bart's parents who had taken over a year to pay the family dental bill—and even then only after he had been forced to hire a collection agency to badger them. No one had been more relieved than Osborne when the elder Mrs. Nystrom had called to tell him he was fired as their family dentist, harrumphing that they would take their business to "a much better dentist—that nice, young Roger Metternich." Roger didn't get paid either.

But family tradition aside, there was no proof that Bart was attempting to swindle Catherine Higgins. So a better approach might be to suggest that an honest mistake may have been made: Bart's recently deceased father, Ernie, must have neglected to inform his son that Ernie had promised to sell

Dr. Higgins' oak instrument cabinet on consignment. Simple as that.

But he would have to launch that option with hand signals in hopes that the women—Dr. Higgins' widow, Catherine, and Osborne's daughter, Erin—would keep quiet even though he knew they would strongly disagree. Given that the value of antique oak cabinets had skyrocketed with the debut of *Antiques Roadshow*, both were convinced Bart had hidden the furniture thinking that eighty-six-year-old Catherine would forget about it, which she certainly had not.

"I remember the day my husband brought it here in our old station wagon," Catherine had said, "and I have never received any money from your shop so it can't have been sold. Now you have already pushed me out of here once and called me a lunatic but I'm back, and I'm back with my lawyer here and her father, Dr. Paul Osborne, who was one of my husband's friends *and a dentist*—so he knows exactly what that cabinet looks like!"

"You should listen to Mrs. Higgins," Erin had said, "or I could slap a lien on your store until the matter is resolved."

Osborne had said nothing, well aware that his presence as a tall male, a Loon Lake professional, was enough.

And so it was that the three of them, by refusing to move from the steps of the Nystrom Antiques Emporium, had forced Bart to surrender—though not with grace.

All he did was yank open the door to the basement as he said: "If you're so damn sure, go see for yourselves. And you be careful you don't damage anything down there either."

Once on their way down the rickety basement steps, he had slammed the door shut, leaving them in the gloom of the crammed storage area with only a few hanging bulbs to light the way.

That was two hours ago. So far no sign of the oak cabinet. Yet, in spite of the stumbling over boxes and the scraping of knees and elbows on ancient chiffoniers, Osborne knew the two women would not give up until they had inspected every inch of the place.

Catherine Higgins was Erin's first client in her new probate law practice and Erin was anxious to do everything she could to help the elderly woman settle her late husband's estate. The missing furniture was an emotional issue for the widow; her husband had insisted on consigning the cabinet to the antiques store in spite of her objections. He didn't realize the sentimental value it had for his wife and their adult children.

Erin had promised to get it back. Having passed the Bar just two months earlier, she might be faulted for lack of experience, but not determination.

Nor was Catherine herself a pushover. Frail in body, the old woman was quite spry in mind and not willing to back away from a fight. It didn't help that she had initially approached Bart on her own and had been rudely treated: "Kicked me right out his front door," she'd said with the fervor of a woman half her age.

What worried Osborne most at this moment was that if the cabinet didn't surface soon, both women might dress Bart down—leaving them all in an untenable position.

He had a brainstorm as he edged closer to the feathers. One that might ease the tension: *what if he bought something from the shop?* Osborne reached into his shirt pocket for his reading glasses to get a better view of what appeared to be a tail fan from a partridge or a pheasant. If it was in good condition and he offered to buy it—that might appease Bart *and* improve the décor of his screened-in porch. Everyone complained he didn't have enough pictures up.

Osborne nodded, pleased with that idea. And if Erin and Catherine did manage to find the cabinet, then a modest purchase on his part could go a long way towards making the morning a "win-win" for all parties. Funny how a day goes, he thought. The last thing on his mind earlier that morning had been shopping for antiques.

——•◦•——

It was Erin who had caught up with him during his morning coffee klatch with his buddies at McDonald's. "Please, Dad," she'd said after pulling him aside to explain Catherine's dilemma, "you know you can intimidate that Bart Nystrom better than I ever could. And I have got to find a way to search that shop."

"Ah, the old 'fear of the dentist' trick, is that it?" asked Osborne, flattered that she had confidence in his patient management skills even though he was a good two years into retirement. Or maybe it was that he was a foot taller and had thirty years on the guy?

"No, Dad, this has nothing to do with dentistry. You're dating the chief of police. That counts."

"Oh," said Osborne, hesitant to share a concern that had been bothering him all week: the police chief in question, Lewellyn Ferris, was getting ready for her high school reunion, and she had not invited him to come along.

"Doc, you know these things are boring as hell for people who weren't there," Lew had said. He wanted to disagree but the tone of her voice made it clear her mind was made up. Later, Lew had shared the fact that she was invited to the Friday night fish fry by an old high school boyfriend—a well-to-do homebuilder from outside Madison, apparently a millionaire, who was recently divorced. Osborne didn't want to tell Erin that as of next Monday he might not be dating the chief of police.

"Dad, is something wrong? You look so glum," Erin had said as they drove to pick up Catherine Higgins.

"Oh, heavens, no," said Osborne. Erin shot him a quick look. She knew something was up.

———

And so Osborne, Erin and Catherine had found themselves in the dust and gloom searching for the instrument cabinet that had graced the dental office of the late Dr. Walter Higgins. Walt had been a favorite of Osborne's—a skilled practitioner and a man with whom he had spent many enjoyable hours fishing, not to mention carpooling together to attend Wisconsin State Dental Society meetings.

If doing his best to intimidate Bart into letting Erin and Walt's widow into the storeroom was one way to memorialize his friend, Osborne was happy to oblige. Maybe playing the heavy would take his mind off Lewellyn, her reunion party to which he was not invited, and the millionaire homebuilder. No such luck.

Reading glasses perched on his nose, Osborne shouldered his way past a towering pine armoire that was the last antique preventing his getting a good look at the feathers protruding from the rug. As he got closer, he could see the fan was an odd mix of black and grey feathers, some streaked umber. Definitely not from a partridge. Goose? Bald eagle? If the latter, Bart was in trouble: unless you are Native American, it is illegal to possess feathers from a bald eagle.

On the other hand, this could be the remains of a bird who flew in the wrong window. Wouldn't surprise Osborne. The musty cavern through which they had been picking their way had already proven to be the final resting place for numerous mice and one desiccated squirrel whose corpse was stained onto the cushions of an old sofa.

Osborne knelt to get a good look at the fan. He tugged at the edge of the rug, which fell away in his hand. Empty eyes stared up at him with teeth bared. Osborne stared back speechless. Those weren't feathers—that was hair.

"Hey, Dad, we found it!" cried Erin from across the room. "The cabinet is here and it's not too heavy. C'mon. You and I can move it easily."

Osborne tried to answer but no words came out as the skull rolled out of the rug and onto the wooden floor.

CHAPTER 2

Breath held, Mason arched back, heels digging into the sand along the edge of the pond. She had managed to set the hook and now she resisted the urge to yank on the reel as the fish bent the spinning rod down, down. Waiting for the right moment she tensed, then, fingers strong, she reeled her prize into the shallow water hoping, hoping …

Darn.

The last fish she wanted to catch was another big, fat bullhead. Not even her grandpa was willing to struggle with knives and pliers to clean one of those. Darn, darn, and darn! She dropped to her knees to wriggle the hook out of the fish's mouth.

All morning she had been hoping to catch a stringer of perch or sunfish or crappie. Now it was almost lunchtime and she'd had no luck. Mason eased the hook out and guided the bullhead back into the pond. Sitting back on her heels, she gave a sigh as she watched the fish swim off to scarf someone else's worms.

Not ready to give up, she turned to reach for the cottage cheese container holding her night crawlers. Her eye caught movement in the distance: across the river on the island. Something pale and pink in the sunlight like a giant sausage standing on end. Bouncing, kind of. What on earth?

Mason set her worms down and peered across the road, one hand shielding her eyes from the high morning sun as she strained to get a better look. Standing at the far end of the pond made it hard to see past the bushes along the river.

———•——

The Jaycee Kiddie Fish Pond was a kidney-shaped, manmade water hole situated east of the dirt road that ran along the Wisconsin River. It ended at a railroad trestle that fed boxcars into the paper mill. Every spring the Jaycees stocked the pond with panfish, hoping more youngsters might learn to enjoy the sport that fueled state revenues. But bullheads had crashed the party, so interest was limited. That sunny summer morning, eight-year-old Mason was the only kid fishing. And no adults were allowed.

Beyond the road was a narrow strip of grass that ended at the river's edge. The river ran deep with a strong current that swirled around a small island about thirty yards straight across from the road. An outpost of straggly jack pine, clumps of tag alders and flotsam left after the spring floods, the island was uninhabited. The only access was by the train tracks running across the trestle.

The railway, which was suspended over rapids visible between the ties, had no guardrail. Though Loon Lake teenagers were known to dare one another to cross, no one Mason's age was brave enough to even consider getting close.

The Jaycees had put up a barbed wire fence to close it off, but people or animals had bent it forward—it could be crossed if one were determined.

————•————

Mason took a few steps along the edge of the pond, hoping for a better look at whatever that was out on the island. Fishing here almost every day since school got out, she had seen some of the big boys out there fooling around but nothing that color, and such a weird shape. Again she raised one hand over her brow and squinted into the sun.

At first it didn't register. Then her breath caught. Now she saw. And the awful boy saw her. She whirled around, a scream catching in her throat as she scrambled for her things. Grabbing her rod, she threw the worms into the pail with her tackle box and clutching the pail to her chest, she ran. Feet pounding up the road she dared a glance across the river. The boy was gone.

She ran and ran, unable to keep from sobbing. Along the road up to River Street, then five blocks to cross Wisconsin Avenue and down past the Masonic Temple. When she was three blocks from home, she was so out of breath she had to stop. She looked back: A bike two blocks away and heading towards her. She couldn't see the rider. No time to make it home.

The big house on the corner—their garage door was open. She ducked, scuttling along the fence, hoping it would hide her. Inside the garage she crouched behind a garbage can and waited, barely breathing. A clicking noise … then the patter of footsteps. She pressed back hard against the wall of the garage.

Too late she realized she was hold the spinning rod upright.

CHAPTER 3

"Yeah, hey, Mr. Calvertson? You home? Curt—" Standing at the bottom of the stairs, Ron Shradtke shouted up at the deck of the log home. The late June morning had warmed the air so only a screen door separated the outside from the inside of the big house. Ron started up the stairs but Kenny tugged on his shirt, stopping him. "Look at your boots, man, they're filthy."

"Oh yeah," said Ron, backing down to where his friend stood. The screen door swung open.

"Calverson—the name is *Cal-VER-son* for Chrissake—how many times do I have to tell you goombahs?" Curt Calverson walked over to the deck railing, coffee cup in hand, and looked down.

He was dressed in the crisp khakis and open-necked white button-down shirt of a northwoods businessman prepped for casual Friday. Didn't matter to Kenny how the guy was dressed—or the fact he was clean-shaven with his hair combed back so soft and smooth. None of that could disguise the small head with its pockmarked face and skin the color of liver: just add a tail and Kenny'd swear the guy was a lizard.

Annoyance on his face, Curt returned the stares of the two men. "Whaddya want?"

"Well … we're here to get paid," said Ron, glancing back towards Kenny to include him in the request. Kenny had sidled up to stand behind Ron but at an angle, as if looking over his shoulder and ready to run. No matter what Ron said, Kenny Reinka couldn't help feeling skittish around Calverson. He worried every time he had to deal with him. But then, Kenny was short and wiry while Ron, hell, he had muscle on him. Fact was that without Ron's strength—and his equipment—they would never have been able to log that back forty for the guy.

Curt reached into his left shirt pocket for a pack of cigarettes, shook one out with one hand, set his coffee mug on the deck railing, and searched his pants pocket for a lighter. "That's right, Ron, you left me a couple-a voice mails 'bout this, didn't you."

"Yep, we finished logging that whole section just like you asked. I don't see them logs piled up back in there so I take it they got delivered and you got paid."

"That I did." Curt pulled on his cigarette and exhaled slowly. He said nothing.

"Well …"

"The way I see it you boys were pulling down unemployment that whole time, right?"

"Yeah … so? What's that got to do with it?" asked Ron, a tremor of anger in his voice.

Ron wasn't just strong, he was *big*, with shoulders so broad he had to buy flannel shirts that hung to his knees. He was wearing a green and black checked one today along with baggy jeans that slopped over his beat-up work boots. A rough, black beard might hide most of his face but not the eyes, and Kenny knew his friend's eyes would be burning now. Beard or no beard, anyone could see right away when Ron was mad.

Kenny resisted the urge to scramble back to the safety of his pickup, hoping to hell things wouldn't get worse. If they did, he wouldn't be much help. He was only five-five and weighed less than a hundred and forty. Not built for bar fights.

"It's okay, Ron, we can take care of this later," said Kenny, pulling on Ron's sleeve for the second time. Ron shrugged him off.

"I said 'what's that got to do with it,' *Calvertson*." Kenny was sure Ron deliberately mispronounced the guy's name. Like that helps. "We logged that back forty of yours and now we're here to get paid." Ron set his shoulders and returned Curt's stare.

"That's called 'double dipping,' my man," said Curt. "Against the law. IRS'll be after you."

"The hell they will—this is under the table, you know that."

"Yes I do. You want me to blow the whistle?"

*"Are you saying you're not gonna pay us?"* Incredulity rang in Ron's voice.

Now even Kenny was surprised. He was expecting the guy to hassle them down a few bucks. But not pay them anything?

"How many times I gotta repeat myself?" Curt knocked an ash off his cigarette. "Bye, boys." He walked back into the house, the screen door slamming behind him.

Speechless, Ron turned around, then turned again as if ready to run up the stairs.

"Hey, man, forget it," said Kenny, pulling him towards the pickup. "I don't need this shit—you don't either. The guy's a jackass. We can take care of it—we can make damn sure nobody works for that asshole ever again."

"I'll make sure of more than that," said Ron, climbing into the passenger seat and slamming the door hard.

"Hey, easy on my truck," said Kenny. "Look, we got twenty minutes before we gotta be back on the road crew—let me buy you a beer. Calm us both down."

"Don't want a beer."

"You don't want a gun either or you'll end up back in the hoosegow," said Kenny, angling for a little humor.

But Ron wasn't buying. Hunched forward, his face closed in, he was silent. As the pickup sped down the county highway, Kenny glanced from the corner of his eye. Ron's lower jaw was working. Never a good sign.

That Calverson is one lucky guy, thought Kenny as the two men drove in silence back to the road construction crew that was their employment seven months of the year. He's lucky Bobby Shradtke is still doing hard time or sure as hell Ron would be calling on his big brother for help just like he did when they were kids.

Kenny remembered those days all right. Big Bobby was always there for Ron, which is why to this day guys stayed out of his way. Kenny was still in the service when Bobby got sent away, but he had been informed of the circumstances. Circumstances he heard once and never wanted to hear again.

"Yep," said Kenny, attempting to lighten the dead air between them, "he sure is lucky Big Bobby ain't around."

Ron looked down at the floorboards of the pickup, then swiveled his head to grin at Kenny. "Who said he's not around? I didn't say that. Did you hear me say that?"

CHAPTER 4

Erin and Catherine peered over Osborne's shoulder as he used his pen to tip the skull from one side to the other. A touch of gold caught light in the dim room.

"Isn't *that* interesting," he said, leaning closer only to pause, then sit back on his heels, "but I better wait before examining this further. The light in here is lousy, and the last thing I need to do is compromise any evidence that the Wausau boys might be able to use."

"Why, Dad? You think that skull is human?" Erin spoke in a whisper, her eyes wide.

"Without question."

"Oh dear," said Catherine, adjusting her glasses for a closer look. "Things are so old here." She touched the far end of the rug, which was still rolled tight. "Thick with dust—this hasn't been moved in ages. Maybe it's from a museum?"

Osborne shrugged, "only Bart can answer that question, but we aren't the people to ask." He got to his feet.

"Now why did you say 'Wausau boys,' Dr. Osborne?" said Catherine, "what on earth does Wausau have to do with this?"

Osborne repressed the urge to be short with the elderly woman. He wasn't in the mood to provide a complete profile of the workings—or non-workings—of the Loon Lake Police Department.

"They run the crime lab for our region," said Osborne. "Since Chief Ferris has only two full time police officers and a couple deputies she can call on—like myself or Ray Pradt—Loon Lake needs their lab services whenever there's a crime requiring more science than what's available here."

———

Was it Lew canceling their weekly Wednesday morning coffee (the one his McDonald's buddies kidded him about) that put him in such bad humor? The more he dwelt on it, the more it bothered him. Not the reunion so much as that homebuilder guy. And the fish fry.

And not just any Friday night fish fry but one with former classmates and … *and* that homebuilder guy. Lew was honest about the guy, saying she'd had a crush on him sophomore year. The same guy who was recently retired, divorced and worth millions. She also said he had started emailing her last month, letting her know he was coming for the reunion. Osborne knew exactly what that jerk must have in mind.

No wonder he was doing his best to keep any discussion of Loon Lake Police Chief Lewellyn Ferris to a minimum.

———

"But I thought that's what we pay Dr. Pecore for," said Catherine, unwilling to drop the subject. "I see his wife at the beauty shop every Friday and she's always complaining that he has to work so hard. He's the coroner, isn't he? Isn't that what coroners do? Make decisions on dead bodies?"

"Pecore may allege to be a pathologist but his level of competence extends to determining if someone's dead or alive—period," said Osborne. "And that's assuming he's not dead drunk at the time."

"Yeah, Dad, don't hold back," said Erin. She tipped her head to look at him, "Dad, *what* is eating your shorts today?"

Osborne gave her the dim eye. She winked back. Pursing his lips and saying nothing, Osborne pointed the two women in the direction of the cabinet. Following behind, he said, "I don't mean to be unkind, Catherine, but you know what they call the guy who graduates at the bottom of his class in med school, don't you? M.D."

"I understand," said Catherine, "Dr. Pecore is not your favorite person."

"This is true. Drives me nuts taxpayers have to pay for his incompetence." Dumping on Pecore boosted Osborne's spirits enough that in spite of what he knew would make him a better person, he decided to deliver a full dose: "You heard about the dogs, right?"

"The dogs?" asked Catherine, stopping to turn a puzzled look his way. "I don't believe I have."

"Well, that razzbonya was letting his golden retrievers hang out in the autopsy lab. Think about that for a minute.

Think how families of the dearly departed like to hear someone they love has been nuzzled by canines."

"That's disgusting," said Catherine.

"Darn right it is," said Osborne, letting the rant relieve even more of his frustration.

Erin, who had heard the story numerous times, listened with a grin on her face. "Don't stop now, Dad," she said.

"I've said enough," said Osborne, catching himself from saying more with a sheepish smile.

"What Dad hasn't said is that Pecore got the job and keeps the job because he's married to our mayor's wife's sister. Local politics trumps taxpayer rights every time.

"On the other hand, if Pecore weren't such a screw-up, Dad wouldn't be the dental forensics go-to guy for Chief Ferris—and for the Wausau boys. Right, Dad? It's in your best interest that Pecore Velcroes his butt to a bar stool. Means you get a second career as a part time odontologist—and a girlfriend to boot. Right?"

"Now the girlfriend part I *have* heard," Catherine said, with a chuckle that proved that even at the age of eighty-six one is never too old for good gossip.

"All right, Erin," said Osborne, "enough of this or I won't help you ladies get your furniture out of here." He stared down at the oak instrument chest before glancing up at his daughter. "Think you and I can manage to move this ourselves?"

Picking up one end of the cabinet, Osborne was surprised to find it lighter than he expected. Erin grasped the other end and together they lifted it easily. "Okay," said Osborne, "but set it down for a minute. One thing I have to do before we move it—do you have your cell phone with you?"

"Sure, Dad, but where's yours?"

"Out in the car."

"Dad, are you kidding me? You're supposed to have it with you all the time—isn't that why the Loon Lake Police Department pays the bill?"

"Erin," said Osborne, adopting the tone he used when she was a youngster who had to be reminded to brush her teeth, "I'm wearing my pager. That's enough electronics for one man."

"Not if he's a deputy police officer. D-a-a-d, you need to carry that phone. This is an excellent example why. Right now, right here."

"You're right. You're absolutely right," said Osborne, the crankiness of the morning descending again. He had deliberately not worn the phone so that he wouldn't be tempted to call Lew and pester her with questions that were none of his business. Questions like 'Does this homebuilder jabone have all of his own teeth? Has he any concept of a fly rod? Maybe he's allergic to fresh air. Maybe he's too out of shape to wade …' Questions that were none of his business for sure.

"Now—can I make the call?" He held out one hand.

With a shake of her head and a grimace of exasperation, Erin reached for her cell phone, which she wore attached to her belt. She tossed it to Osborne.

CHAPTER 5

Marlene, on the switchboard in the Loon Lake Police Department, answered his call. She listened then said, "Doc, Chief Ferris is in meetings with probation officers until one p.m. I can patch you through if this is an emergency."

"Use your judgment, Marlene. The victim isn't going anywhere fast, believe me. But this is a skeletal remain, it is human, it is in a place of business and I do need direction on what to do next."

Seconds later, the voice that lifted his heart no matter the frustrations of their relationship came on the line: "Yeah, Doc, Marlene said you found a body at Nystrom's shop? An accident? What's the story?" Lew's tone was clipped and urgent.

"Not a body, a human skull—but it's been here a while. Years from the look of it, Lew, so no reason to leave your meeting and rush over. I just need to know how to handle the situation with Bart Nystrom. And, Lew, this may be nothing. Could be part of a cadaver from a medical school—"

"But it is human, right?"

Oh, yes, I am sure of that."

"Okay, Doc. Tell Bart to close up shop and not let anyone in until I can get there, which won't be until around two or a little later. Make it clear that order includes Bart as well."

"Last question, Lew. Erin's client found a cabinet that belongs to her and she wants it back. It's in a section of the storeroom a good distance from the skull. Is there a problem if I help the ladies move that?"

"If moving it doesn't damage the chain of custody for any evidence related to the other finding, I see no reason why you shouldn't. Are you available to meet me out there later?"

"Certainly." Now came the familiar rush of guilt tempered with a light heart. Crime scenes might be sad scenes for most people, but not for Dr. Paul Osborne. Not only did they give him an excuse to stay current with forensic dentistry and the profession he had loved—but they promised more time with a woman he wished he could see every day.

Osborne handed the phone back to Erin, saying, "Thank you, hon. Let's you and me move that cabinet and then I have bad news for Bart."

————◦•◦————

Bart's face morphed into a crimson moon when Osborne told him to close up shop. Without saying a word, he spun around and headed for the door to the basement. Storming down the stairs, he paused to hit a light switch that illuminated the storeroom quite nicely.

"Wonder where *that* was for the last two hours," mused Osborne as he hurried after Bart who was bumping and shoving his way through dust-burdened, rickety stacks of chairs, headboards, dressers and tables.

"Where the hell is that thing?" said Bart, his big head swinging back and forth as his eyes scanned the back of the storeroom. "That rug in the corner—that it?"

"I wouldn't go there, Bart," said Osborne. "I relayed Chief Ferris's instructions: do not touch anything until she gets here. This may be a crime scene."

"The hell it is," said Bart, pushing the tall armoire so hard it tipped sideways onto a nearby desk. He stared down at the rolled up rug and the skull on the floor. "Goddamn bear skull is what you're lookin' at. My old man had some taxidermy crap that he couldn't get rid of so he stored it back here."

———⋅◦⋅———

Osborne understood Bart's reasoning: the skeleton of a bear so closely resembles that of a human being that local game wardens and law enforcement officials anticipate several calls a month from hikers or hunters convinced they've stumbled onto a dead body. Ninety-nine percent of the time the bones are bear, not human.

Before Osborne could stop him, Bart had yanked at the rug, rolling it back to expose a jumble of skeletal remains.

———⋅◦⋅———

"Bart!" Osborne reached for the man's arm, which he held tight, "don't move another inch or you'll find yourself under arrest."

The two men stared in silence at the contents of the rug. Whoever it was did not appear to have arrived in one piece. The interior of the old rag rug was stained black in the areas surrounding the bones. Time had not erased traces of decomposition.

"Ohmygod—what the hell *is* this?" said Bart, backing away from the grisly display, nausea knotting his face.

Relieved that the antique dealer was willing to step back and not disturb anything further, Osborne didn't answer. He had his own questions: Had a human being been dismembered? Body parts shoved into this rag rug to decompose?

He spotted a tag on one end of the rug and bent to read it.

"Hey, Bart," he said, "this may help—looks like the tag's got the name of the person who gave your father the rug to sell." As Bart reached for the tag, Osborne grabbed his arm for a second time, "please don't touch that. Could have fingerprints."

"Doc," said Bart, straightening up and shoving his face into Osborne's, "what is it with you? You're not a cop—you're a retired dentist. So just keep your nose the hell out of my business. You hear me? And forget closing my shop. This is tourist season—I have people stopping in ..."

"I hear you, Bart. But if you'll take a minute to listen to me, I'll explain things. No, I am not a police officer, but I am deputized by the Loon Lake Police Department to assist with the forensic investigations on any unnatural deaths."

"Whaddya talking about? That's Pecore's job."

Osborne resisted the urge to punch the guy in the nose. He took a deep breath before answering.

"I do the dental exams."

"So—" said Bart, planting both hands on his hips before waving an arm at Osborne, "Go off and do a goddamn dental exam and leave me alone, will ya?"

"Bart …" Osborne kept his voice firm, "before helping the ladies move their cabinet, I took a good look at this skull."

"And …?" Bart challenged.

"Bears do not have gold fillings, son. Doors closed until two this afternoon."

CHAPTER 6

Human confetti dotted the steps of Erin's front porch: a vivid blur of yellows, blues, greens and orange-reds scattered among the t-shirts, shorts, blue jeans, baseball caps, sneakers and shorts. If Osborne hadn't known it was time for lunch, he would have thought it was already the Fourth of July—with his grandchildren and the neighbor kids waiting for the parade to begin. As it was, they were just waiting for their mom and peanut butter sandwiches.

On the bottom step, tossing a neon green beach ball back and forth with his best friend Ben, was Cody, the youngest of Osborne's grandchildren. Nearly four and the only boy in the family, Cody was as blond as his mother, as slender as both his parents, and already one of the tallest boys in his class.

Two steps above Cody sat Beth, age twelve, and as fair-haired and fair-skinned as her brother—except for the lavender eye shadow, darkened lashes and scarlet cell phone glued to one ear—hints of teendom already vexing her parents. Two neighbor boys, Ben's older brothers, were hunkered off to one side of the porch intent on a handheld video game when they weren't stealing glances at Beth.

Nearly hidden behind Beth was a figure unfamiliar to Osborne: a young woman with a peach fresh face and shoulder-length blond hair pulled tight into a ponytail. Dressed like a runner in a tank top, shorts and sneakers, she sat on the porch step with her knees bent, one arm cradling the shoulders of eight-year-old Mason.

As Osborne got closer to the crowd on the porch he could see that his youngest granddaughter had been crying.

----•◆•----

The sight of Mason with her cap of dark brown hair and face tanned nut-brown by the summer sun never failed to remind Osborne of his own mother, who had died when he was six.

He kept a photo of Mason's great-grandmother on his dresser—a picture taken by the man who had loved her. In the picture she sat, knees tucked under a light summer dress on a blanket laid for a picnic. Every time Osborne let his gaze linger on that photo—his mother's easy smile, her even, white teeth, the strands of dark hair loosened from her bun to blow in a summer breeze—he saw the woman Mason would be someday.

Of all his grandchildren, she was the only one who had inherited the warm, brown skin and the black-brown eyes so similar to his own: evidence of his mother's Metis heritage. Each year the high cheekbones and the broad forehead grew more pronounced in the young girl. Each year her grandfather let his hands rest longer on her shoulders. So long as he lived he would be there for her no matter her mistakes.

———

Right now, those shoulders were hunched as she leaned into the woman beside her. Leaned as if she would hide if she could. Well, thought Osborne, Mason *is* the one kid in Erin's household you can count on for surprises. Wonder what the little rascal has been up to this time?

If he had to guess, he would bet she'd been caught setting off firecrackers—the tiny red ones kids always seem to find even though they're illegal—but a quick scan of the sitting child indicated Mason had all her appendages, no obvious injuries and no blood in sight. Whatever it was couldn't be too serious.

"Oh, jeez, Dad," Erin muttered under her breath as she hurried along the sidewalk behind him. "What's Mason done now?" In a louder voice she called out to the group on the porch: "Hey, sorry to be late, guys. I'll have lunch ready in a few minutes. Beth, you keep an eye on Cody."

Beth threw her mother a look of disgust, "M-o-o-m, what do you think I've been doing all morning." The cell phone never left her ear.

As Osborne made his way up the porch steps—squeezing between Cody and Ben and hoping not to get a beach ball in the head—the young woman next to Mason got to her feet.

"Hi, I'm C.J. Calverson," she said, brushing at strands of hair that had come loose from her ponytail before extending her right hand. The running shorts and tank top exposed the curves of an athlete: upper arms muscled, calves defined, a strong torso. Osborne guessed she couldn't be much over twenty.

"Are you Mason's father?" she asked, worry in her voice.

"No, I'm her grandfather, Dr. Paul Osborne. This is her mother," said Osborne, beckoning towards Erin.

Mason burst into tears.

"Oh, golly, what's wrong, kiddo?" asked Osborne, bending over to peer into the tear-stained face. Erin pushed her way in beside him.

"Mason," said her mother, "Are you hurt? What happened?" Erin turned sideways. "Beth, what's the story here? I left you in charge. Get off the damn phone!"

Beth shrugged and closed her cell phone. "They just got here, Mom. Mason wouldn't tell me anything."

"I found her hiding in my garage," said the woman, extending her hand this time to Erin. "C.J. Calverson."

"Erin Stiles," said Erin, giving the woman's hand a quick shake before turning back to her daughter. "*Hiding in a garage?* What on earth? Mason, tell me what happened."

Osborne stepped up onto the wide porch area and out of Erin's way. Mason shook her head 'no' as she kept sobbing.

"She's been like this since I found her about an hour ago," said C.J. with an expression as perplexed as Erin's. "At first she wouldn't even tell me her name or where she lived. I sure hope you don't mind that I made her come in my kitchen and have a cookie and a glass of orange juice. I just wanted her to settle down a little …"

"Oh, that's okay," Erin said, as she stood up, pulled Mason to her feet and hugged her close before turning back to C.J. "Where did you say you live?"

"Right up the street," said C.J. pointing off to the left. "We're in the process of moving in to that house on the corner—the one kiddie-corner from the court house."

"You mean the old Daniels' place?" said Erin, "that large stucco with the cupola?"

"Yes. We have a summer home on Stone Lake, too. That's where we're staying right now. I had just come to town to pick up some boxes the movers left when I found your daughter."

C.J.'s eyes took on the worried look again, "I tell you, this little girl was shaking she was so scared." She reached over to pat Mason's head. "I've never seen a kid so frightened. Took a while to get her to calm down enough to tell me where she lived."

"Really," said Erin, tipping Mason's tear-stained face up to wipe at her cheeks with a Kleenex. "Mason, honey?" Erin grasped her daughter by the shoulders and tried to make eye contact, but Mason looked down and away. "Won't you tell us what's wrong? Something must have happened. You don't just hide in people's garages."

"No, Mom, really," said Mason, pulling away with a shrug. "I'm okay." She took another Kleenex from her mother and blew her nose while Erin rubbed her shoulders.

"I can see you're *okay*, hon—but that's not what I asked," said Erin. Mason swung her head back and forth, still refusing to answer. She handed the used Kleenex back to her mother and said, "Can I go play with Cody and Ben 'til lunch?"

"Alright—but we are talking later. You hear me?"

"Um-hmm," said Mason as she skipped down the porch steps and scooted towards the back yard with Cody and Ben right behind her.

"That didn't sound too convincing," said Osborne.

Erin watched her go then turned towards C.J. and Osborne. "Dad, you'll stay for lunch, won't you? And, C.J., how about you? Egg salad sandwiches …" Erin beckoned towards the front door.

C.J. checked her watch. "I'm afraid Curt is expecting me back at the lake—"

Erin gave her a quizzical look: "You don't mean Curt Calverson, the CEO of Calverson Finance, do you? Is he your father?"

"My husband."

"Oh!" Erin couldn't hide the surprise in her voice.

"We've just been married a few months," said C.J.

"Oh. Well, I'm sorry to sound so surprised but I happened to be reading about your husband the other day and I assumed—"

"Right, he's a lot older," said C.J. "We met last year. I was his personal trainer." She gave a rueful grin. "Seemed like a good idea at the time."

"Hey, that's okay, whatever works," said Erin, suddenly so friendly Osborne knew she was up to something. "So you're pretty new in town, aren't you?"

"Yeah, gee, I've only been here two weeks. Except for the clerks at the grocery store, I really haven't met many people." The girl sounded wistful.

The slamming of a car door prompted everyone to glance back to the street where a long, lean figure in knee-length khaki shorts and a beard resembling an exploded spaniel was emerging from a battered blue pickup truck. "Yo," called out a deep voice from somewhere within the beard, "don't anyone move!"

He reached into the bed of the truck for an object that he stuck onto his head, then took a moment to check his reflection in the truck window. Satisfied with the jaunty angle of his headpiece, he reached into the truck bed once more. This time he straightened up with yet another prize dangling from his arm: a very long, narrow fish. Still twitching.

Walking around the back end of the truck with the fish held high, he started across Erin's front lawn towards the porch.

"No, you don't, Ray," said Erin in a loud, firm voice. "You stop right there. That muskie is dripping blood all over the place and I do not want it on my porch."

The man paused, chagrin on his face, "but this is a monster mount, Erin—fifty-one inches! I gotta show the kids—"

"Dr. Osborne," said C.J. in a low whisper from where she stood beside Osborne, "what on earth does that man have on his head?"

CHAPTER 7

C.J. giggled, cupping her right hand over her mouth as she tried to eat her egg salad sandwich without spitting. Osborne caught a glance from Erin that confirmed they were both aware that C.J.'s need to catch up with her husband appeared to have vanished with the arrival of a six-foot-six thirty-two-year-old wearing a stuffed trout on his head.

Osborne shook his head as he always did while watching Ray charm the females: who knew that a man who walked with the grace of an accordion folding and unfolding could be so attractive to women? Was it the little kid smile on the face of the grown man? A smile that made you think the sun had just come out—just for you and him? Or was it simply Ray's delight in being alive at this moment?

Whatever it was worked on women of all ages, ethnic origins, sizes, and marital statuses—from bait shop clerks to heiresses to women of faith. Yep, even the nuns at St. Mary's adored the guy.

"So where can I buy a hat like that?" asked C.J., wiping her mouth with her napkin, "I know somebody who'd love one."

"Well ... you can't buy one," said Ray as he reached for a
handful of black olives and baby carrots from the relish plate
that Erin had set in the middle of the kitchen table. "A friend
made it for me. Margaret Taggert ... a grand gal who passed
away a couple years ago ... and *that* is too bad. I've had l-o-
o-ts of people ask me where they can get a hat just like mine.
I tell ya ... Margaret could have made a few bucks. "

The hat in question was currently resting just above eye
level on Cody's head, Cody having appointed himself the
hat's official custodian upon any visit of Ray's to their home—
an appointment that usually led to protests from Mason. But
Mason had not objected today. Used to the kids' bickering,
Osborne found that odd.

At the moment, Cody sported the summer version of the
worn leather cap: ear flaps tucked up so that the head and tail
of the fish protruded so far over his ears that the hat was in
danger of taking up an extra place at the kitchen table. Under
the kitchen lights, the antique wood and metal fishing lure
draped across the breast of the stuffed trout sparkled as
brightly as C.J.'s eyes every time she stole a glance at Ray.

"So, Ray, just how old was Margaret Taggert before she
passed away?" Osborne asked.

"Ninety-two. Both Margaret and old Ike were ninety-two.
Margaret ... died first and Ike ... just twenty hours later. Hard
to believe, y'know. But old Ike ... he was in the nursing home
when he was told she'd gone to heaven, and that was that.
They were a pair those two—raised green beans, tomatoes,

Brussels sprouts and sweet peas right up until the end. A real love story ..."

"Ray drove the Taggerts to town for all their doctor visits," said Osborne in answer to the quizzical look on C.J.'s face. "Margaret came up with the idea for that hat all on her own— she knew what would make this razzbonya happy."

"You drove two elderly people in that rattletrap pickup?" C.J. looked horrified.

"I wish," said Osborne with a rueful grin. "Ray lives next door to me so when they needed a ride, he would borrow my car. The more I think about it—I'm the one who deserved the hat." He gave Ray a look of mock anger. The conversation was lifting his spirits in spite of his concern over Lew's millionaire homebuilder.

"All right, you two, stop the squabbling and finish up," said Erin as she started to clear the table. "Cody, give Ray back his hat."

"Hey, Cody," said Ray as he reached for his hat, "what did the one wood tick say to the other wood tick?"

Cody grinned and shook his head, "I dunno."

"Shall we walk or take a fisherman?" Cody gave Ray a blank stare. Mason giggled, Beth looked bored and C.J. stared at Ray for a long moment before chuckling.

"Oh-h-h, no," groaned Erin. "You can do better than that."

Lifting an eyebrow, Ray leaned sideways towards Beth. "So, young lady," he said, "I hear you're about to turn thirteen. I assume your mom has told you the secret to safe sex—"

"Ray …" Erin did not smile. "Do not be inappropriate."

"You're the one who wants a better joke."

"Beth, Cody, Mason, leave the kitchen. Out!" said their mother. With reluctance, the kids got to their feet. A push from their mother got them out of the kitchen through the door to the backyard.

"All right, what's the punch line of this bad joke?" Erin asked, leaning against the kitchen counter with her arms folded, a testy look directed at Ray.

"Make sure the car doors are locked."

"Honestly, Ray, that isn't even funny."

With a grin, Ray shrugged. "I tried." C.J. laughed and he winked at her. Then he got to his feet to help Erin move dishes to the sink.

"So I've got some interesting news," he said. "You heard Loon Lake is going to host the North American Ice Fishing Circuit Championship this winter, right?"

"I didn't know that," said Osborne. "Right here on *our* Loon Lake?" He nodded at C.J. and said, "Wisconsin has fourteen Loon Lakes."

"Yep, but you had to qualify last year."

"Oh. Guess that means none of us can fish it?"

"Well, yeah, but that's not all bad. I got three calls this morning from pros asking me to help 'em learn the honey holes. I'll charge good money for that, too, doncha know."

"Like how much?" asked Erin, reaching for the plate in front of C.J., who refused to take her eyes off Ray. Osborne had to admit his neighbor was looking particularly good in crisp khaki shorts and a dark green T-shirt. But it wasn't until he carried the kids' milk glasses to the sink that they could see the orange lettering across the back of the shirt, which read: "Why are men are like ceramic tile? If you lay 'em right, you can walk over 'em for years."

"Did Mrs. Taggert make your shirt, too?" asked C.J.

"Ah, no," said Ray, turning around with a chuckle. Osborne suspected it was a gift from a former girlfriend. Ray chose to answer Erin's question instead: "Oh, I'm thinking a hundred bucks an hour or so. What do you think? Erin? Doc?"

"That's a lot of money for a guy who makes ten bucks an hour digging graves," said Erin.

"You dig graves?" said C.J., her eyes widening.

"Only … when the fishing is … slow," said Ray, sitting back down in his chair, thrusting out his long legs and settling into a speech pattern he knew would drive Osborne and Erin nuts. "I … happen to have multiple … pursuits and my … 'cemetery responsibilities' … are likely to come off my list this year.

"That is …" he waved an index finger, which Osborne recognized as the Ray Pradt signal that he was about to deliver words of wisdom, if not national importance, "… if a … par-tic-u-lar new opportunity works out … as … I believe it will. Could be … I'll end the winter … *ahead* so to speak."

"And that *new opportunity*—is that the guiding?" Osborne asked, checking his watch. It was nearly time to head back to Nystrom's for the meeting with Lew.

"O-o-o-h-h-h, no," said Ray, each vowel elongated for maximum impact. "*Ice Men* is what it is." Sitting up and splaying his hands across the kitchen table, he dropped the slow cadence to say, "a new reality show that is going to be shot up here. Auditions are being held here next week and ..." he lifted both eyebrows as he grinned, "I'm all signed up."

"You mean *you* could be on TV?" said C.J.

"I surely could. On the Sportsman's Channel, no less. And *that*..."—another wave of the index finger—"is a gig made for me."

"A *jig*, did you say?" said Erin,teasing. She tipped her head towards C.J., "You fish walleyes with a jig. Ray's a walleye expert—aren't you, Ray?"

"You heard me, Erin. I'm not kidding—a *gig* is what I said. Paid work ... fame ... fortune ... all the good stuff. Seriously," said Ray, leaning forward on his elbows, "this could be my big break."

"Wow!" said C.J. "That is s-o-o-o exciting." The expression in her eyes had to make Ray's day. Osborne repressed a smile as she checked her watch, "Oh gosh! I better get going. Curt is going to wonder ..."

"Before you leave," said Erin, "tell me how I can reach you. I am so worried about Mason. If I can get her to talk about whatever it was that scared her this morning, I might have a few questions for you." She handed C.J. a piece of paper for her to write down her number. Erin turned to her father, and frustration clouded her face. "Dad, would you see if *you* can get her to talk? She tells you more stuff than she ever tells me or her dad ..."

"I'll do my best, Erin," said Osborne, "but it'll have to be after I help Lew with the situation at Bart Nystrom's place. I'll stop back around four or so—take her for ice cream."

"Doc," said Ray, "aren't you going to the class reunion with Chief Ferris tonight? I heard they're having pizza and beer out at Smokey's for the early arrivals. Can't believe you're not going."

"I wasn't invited."

"Oh. Sorry I mentioned it." A look of chagrin crossed Ray's face.

"So *that's* why you've been so glum," said Erin, "I could tell something was wrong."

"I'm not glum," said Osborne. "Reunions are of interest only to the people who went to school together. You know that."

Ray and Erin stared at him.

"Believe me, it's not an issue," said Osborne with a wave of his hand. "Lew has lots of old friends to catch up with and she doesn't need to be bothered with me."

"Right, okay," said Ray, sounding less than convinced.

"Hey, I have an idea," said C.J. from where she stood in the doorway, not quite having left yet. "Dr. Osborne, why don't you bring Mason out to our lake house this afternoon? I'll take her tubing and we'll have some fun. Maybe that'll change her mood a little—who knows?

"How 'bout you, Ray? Would you like to join us? I'd love you to meet my husband—he's been looking to hire a good fishing guide ..."

CHAPTER 8

Pulling onto the street, foot heavy on the gas, Osborne headed
south. He was determined to get back to the Nystrom Antiques Emporium by two, if not earlier. If he was lucky, Lew might
have a few extra minutes to chat. With that in mind, he decided
to think positive: what if she changed her mind and decided it
*would* be nice to have him tag along this evening?

The thought was not out of order. After all, how many afternoons had she surprised him with an unexpected phone call:
"Doc, I've got two deputies on duty right now and the day is
too glorious to work. Let's go fishing!"

His mood brightening, Osborne was four blocks down from
Erin's house and slowing for the stoplight when he happened to
glance off to his right at a squalid matchbox of a house. A sham-
bles of peeling paint, warped shingles, crumbling eaves caved in
over a back porch and a rusted out, once-white pickup in the
driveway, it was a house and a truck he had seen a million times.
But today another vehicle was parked behind the pickup. A vehicle he knew too well.

The house was typical of others in Loon Lake that had been built in the early nineteen hundreds for workers employed at the once-thriving paper mill: each a squared-off single story home with an average of five rooms. The largest room would be a kitchen, opening to a small living room that had doors leading to a couple bedrooms and one bath.

Though the exterior of the little house was in desperate need of a paint job, a narrow border of grass nestled between the house and a crumbling rock wall bordering the sidewalk meant something to someone: pristine clay pots of pink petunias spilled their blooms like offered prayers at the feet of two stone figurines.

The cracked concrete walkway leading up to the front door was blessed with the presence of a three-foot high statue of the Virgin Mary, head bowed and hands folded in prayer, the blue of her mantle long faded from the sun. At the far end of the border and facing the street was a brown-robed St. Francis of Assisi, a tiny sparrow poised on the fingertips of his left hand, a birdbath cradled in his right. Two religious icons that many residents of Loon Lake, Osborne included, found ironic; neither had been able to buttress the house from the evils occurring within.

Osborne knew the homeowner as a fellow parishioner at St. Mary's Catholic Church. Edna Shradtke might be in her seventies but she never missed Mass on Sundays, six-thirty a.m. rain or snow, sitting year after year at the same end of the same pew, a pew two rows down from Osborne's. So it was that every Sunday morning he followed her slow walk up to the Communion rail and back. She never drank from the chalice, nor did he.

Widowed thirty years now, Edna was unusually tall for a woman of her generation. Bone-thin with facial features that Osborne found slightly askew due to the angle and crook of her nose—the result of its having been broken several times during her marriage to a short, thick man who had been known to beat her and their four children nightly before he had the good grace to fall out of his fishing boat one night dead drunk.

The beatings were known town-wide because they could be heard by the neighbors. But what Osborne didn't know until after he had lost his wife was that one of Edna's sons had once attempted to molest his eldest daughter, Mallory. While he may not have known of that incident until years after it had occurred, he knew plenty about the man who did it: Bobby Shradtke. And he sure as hell knew Bobby's car.

The unexpected sight of that car for the first time in years triggered a memory of such impact that Osborne had to pull over. He held his breath as his mind churned through the details of a conversation he would never forget—and made a connection so disturbing he felt sick to his stomach.

———

Twenty-three years ago, the driver of that car had followed nine-year-old Mallory home from the Loon Lake skating rink one January night. Osborne and his wife had not yet built their lake home, so the family lived in town just three blocks from the rink. A polite child, Mallory was careful to follow parental instructions and address adults as "Mr." or "Mrs." no matter who they were. Grown-ups were grown-ups—to be treated with respect.

So when the man in the red car asked directions to the Loon Lake Pub she did her best to answer until he opened his door, exposed himself and tried to drag her inside—all the while hee-hawing in a strange, high whinny, a noise which Mallory told Osborne still gives her nightmares.

---

His car stopped at the curb across the street from Edna's home, Osborne stared at the vehicle in the driveway. He was sure it was the same one: a red 1960 Ford Sunliner convertible with a white top. While the tailfins, chrome and hulking size might spark fond memories among some car buffs, he felt only a mounting nausea.

The longer he looked, the more he was sure: that expression on Mason's face, her refusal to tell her mother what had frightened her this morning. Mallory had behaved just like that after the episode with the stranger in the car.

He remembered how he and Mary Lee had known something was up that night when Mallory dashed into the house crying, her shoulders shaking. But she had insisted it was nothing, refusing to answer their questions until they decided she must have had a falling out with one of her little friends and hurried her off to bed. Mary Lee would never know what really happened because Mallory kept her secret for years—until the day after her mother's funeral.

———•◦•———

Mary Lee's death had caught Osborne and their daughters by surprise when a lingering bronchitis turned deadly in the midst of a blinding snowstorm. Even with the Herculean efforts of Ray Pradt—who braved swirling snow and sub-zero temperatures to bolt his plow onto his pickup at two in the morning and rush them to the emergency room (this for a woman who had done her best to get him kicked off his property because his house trailer blocked the view from her dining room window!)—it was too late.

The day following the funeral and the wake, Osborne and his daughters, the three of them reeling from the fatigue that hits after hours and hours of assuaging the grief of friends, opted for a retreat to the woods—far from phones and flowers and casseroles. They stepped into their cross-country skis, slipped on well-stocked backpacks and skied in silence and brilliant sunshine over three miles of fresh powder to Osborne's hunting shack.

In their packs were venison steaks, russet potatoes, two cheeses, crackers and half a case of Leinenkugel Original. In their hearts was a driving need for release from the emotions of the week. And so they drank the beer, grilled the steaks, fried the potatoes, threw salt and pepper on everything, then drank more beer and settled in to talk of Mary Lee the only way they could: through tears and laughter.

Though Osborne had felt *he* was third wheel in his wife's life—a necessary nuisance once their daughters were born—he learned that afternoon that she had held the girls at a distance, too.

"I just never did anything quite right in Mom's eyes," Erin had said with a rueful smile. "Too much of a tomboy when she wanted a princess."

"No, no, that was me," said Mallory.

"W-r-o-o-o-n-g! I was the bad one," said Erin. "You were the model child. You *were* a princess: you always wore the clothes she picked out."

"That's true. I'll give you that," said Mallory. She grinned as she lifted a bottle of beer to her lips, "I remember you buying that prom dress that drove her nuts."

"Ohmygod," said Erin. "I hated the one she wanted me to wear—so I bought one with my own money. I loved the pretty pink polkadots ... strapless ... real low in the back ... and the fact that it was on sale so I couldn't return it. Mom said it made me look like a hooker. She wouldn't let me wear it. Had to wear that yucky green thing of yours or miss the prom."

Erin laughed. "I still like the dress. I have it, you know—hidden back in a closet. Guess now I can wear it for Halloween maybe, huh?"

"That was a darling dress, Erin," said Mallory. "I think the only reason Mom didn't like it was because you didn't let her pick it out. You think she was bad about a dress—try my marriage!"

"Dad, you don't know this, but Mom waited 'til the night before my wedding to tell me I was making a big mistake. As it turns out, she was right—but I wish she had mentioned it earlier, given me some reasons instead of one blunt statement. Life might have been a lot less expensive—I'm still paying my divorce lawyer."

"You think that's bad, let me tell you the time that …" Erin jumped in with another anecdote.

As his daughters had joked and cried through their memories, Osborne had listened with his usual sense of remorse and confusion. He had never been the husband Mary Lee needed, wanted. Never made enough money, never built a house big enough to match her dreams, never moved to a city more sophisticated where he might have had a practice that could pay for a more elegant lifestyle.

A sudden hoot of laughter from Erin as Mallory mimicked her mother yanking Ray Pradt's illegal PVC pipes from the fence near her rose garden caused Osborne to tune back into their conversation. "Mom was furious when she discovered Ray was emptying the sewage from his house trailer back there 'cause he couldn't afford to put in a septic tank. Does he still do that, Dad?"

"Heavens, no. Now, girls, that's enough. Your mother was an opinionated woman, but she loved you. You two were the most important people in her life."

"No, Dad, we weren't," said Mallory with a determined shake of her head, "Mom's bridge club came first—she only really laughed when she was with those women. Think about it."

"Mallory's right, Dad," said Erin. "When it came to us, Mom was always ... aloof. She certainly wasn't touchy-feely, not with me anyway. I just made her crabby."

"Don't argue with us, Dad," Mallory chimed back in as she popped the cap off another Leinenkugel, "I know I'm right because I paid a shrink ten thousand dollars to help me figure it out."

"Mallory, you felt that unloved?" Osborne couldn't believe what he was hearing.

"Kinda like Erin just said—I always thought I was doing something wrong. But I know now that I wasn't really. For reasons that we'll never know, Mom was just short on affection. I suppose that's not the worst thing a parent can do, but I do worry about one thing that may have happened because I was afraid of making her mad ...

"Do you remember the night I ran home from the skating rink? When I was so upset?"

"Yes. You'd been in a fight with one of your friends. You kids were always hitting each other with snowballs—"

"It wasn't that."

And then Mallory told Osborne about how the red car had pulled up, the man asking his questions, talking low so she had to approach the car whereupon he tried to grab her. She was able to pull away but not before he threatened her.

Osborne was stunned. "Wait a minute. That really happened? For heaven's sake, Mallory, why didn't you tell your mother and me?"

"Oh, Dad, it's what we're saying about Mom," said Mallory. "We loved her even if she was always critical. That night I was sure she would say it was my fault. Like I shouldn't have been out so late. Or I must have said something or done something to cause it to happen. Kids … right or wrong, kids think it's their fault. And he did tell me he would kill you and Mom if I said anything."

"Oh, my God," Osborne had said. "All right, I can see not telling your mother. *But me?* Why didn't you tell me?"

"Dad," Mallory had said, tipping her head towards him, "Mom ran the show. Not you.

"But you know what has worried me most all these years? Something I was finally able to work through with my shrink, though it still haunts me: *how many other little kids got hurt by that creep because I didn't say something that night?*"

———›‹———

Osborne accelerated so hard coming out of the intersection his tires spun. Could it be that Bobby Shradtke was out of prison? Molesting youngsters again?

He had to see Lew as soon as possible. Forget the reunion party, he needed advice. A little girl had woken up this morning innocent. Was it already too late? He could only hope she had not been touched.

If she had, then *he* would need help—to keep from doing something he should not do.

CHAPTER 9

Gazing out the window to his left as he sat in Edna Schradtke's living room, Kenny watched the Subaru slow to a stop across the street. He shifted in his chair, hoping to get a good look at the driver, but the sun reflecting off the driver's side windows made it impossible to see. After a long pause, the Subaru drove off. Kenny shrugged. Probably just someone taking a call on a cell phone.

He turned back to the man sitting on the sofa across the room. If eight years of hard time had damaged Big Bobby Schradtke, you sure couldn't see it. He was still six feet tall and all angles—thin as he'd been as a teenager and with that head that looked like it had been in the wrong place when someone slammed a heavy door.

It had struck Kenny years ago that the distance between Bobby's ears was too short while the length of his head from chin to hairline was too long. A hairdo that hinted of a 1950s ducktail didn't help either. Then there were his eyes, which looked like they'd been slipped onto his face kinda sideways.

Yep, Bobby was one weird-looking dude when they were kids, and just as peculiar now. Guys at the bar were always surprised to hear he and Ron were brothers.

———•◦•———

The living room, tidy and spare with the one sofa, two maple end tables holding lamps and three chairs, including Edna's rocker, was stifling in the summer heat despite the open windows. Didn't seem to bother Edna or her parakeet, both of whom were fixated on *Oprah*. So Kenny sat and sweated, watching Edna's fingers weave together a crochet needle and a line of bright red yarn while her sons talked over the sound of the TV as they worked their way through a case of Bud.

"So, Bobby," said Kenny when there was a lull in the brothers' conversation, "what-ah brings you back to Loon Lake? Wouldn't you be better off in Wausau or Green Bay? More jobs for electricians 'round there, I hear." He kept his voice small in the event he was making a mistake just by opening his mouth.

Bobby settled his weird eyes on Kenny, tipped his beer can up for a swig, wiped his mouth, and said in the same spidery voice he'd had as a kid: "Maybe you're right, Kenny. Yep, no doubt you *are* right. Sonofabitch." Bobby sat with his legs akimbo, the left ankle resting on the right knee, right arm thrown across the back of the sofa. "But, man, there is no room in the inn."

"Whaddya mean?" Kenny's question caused Ron to raise a finger in caution and nod towards their mother. Maybe they shouldn't discuss this?

"I mean they got me listed as a sexual predator and no one will rent to me. That's what the hell I mean. Except Ma, right Ma?"

Edna turned calm, sad eyes his way and nodded. She had a solemn grace to her that always surprised Kenny. How had such a quiet woman with her gentle ways given birth to these rough men? Men capable of brutish behavior and foul language—though rarely the latter in Edna's house and even then only Bobby got away with it.

He chalked it up to the old man. He had seen that guy once and made sure to stay out of his way. Even as a little kid, Kenny knew mean when he saw it.

"Bobby," Edna took her eyes off the television screen to gaze at her son, "I want you here. You stay as long as you want. Maybe you'll help me fix the house up a little? Ron never has time, all the logging he's been doing." Her voice was soft, pleading but proud.

"I will, Ma, 'till I make some dough anyway."

Edna studied her oldest son. "Why don't you just plan to make this your home? Keep out of trouble. You need a rest, Bobby. Ron, you tell him."

"Mom loves you best, man," said Ron with a hoot and a swallow of his beer. "You stay here, I'll bet she leaves you the house."

A certain edge in Ron's voice prompted his mother to shoot him a warning look. Then she reached over to pat Bobby's hand, "I want you here. I want you *safe*." The emotion in her voice made it clear to Kenny: Edna did not believe Bobby was guilty of anything.

The elderly woman pushed herself up from the rocker and, one slippered foot after the other, shuffled towards the kitchen. "Excuse me, boys, I need to roll out those cinnamon buns I got rising."

Ron winked at Bobby: "Wha'd I tell you? She's got dementia. There's no damn rolls in the kitchen. I don't let her *near* the stove."

Once she was out of earshot, Bobby set both feet to the floor and leaned forward, shoulders hunched as he braced his elbows on his knees, to whisper to Kenny and Ron. "Gotta tell you something disappoints the hell out of me. Stopped by to give my regards to ol' Rita—Kenny, you remember Rita? She was my ol' lady who finked on me.

"Turns out she passed away last year. What the hell? Diabetes, high blood pressure, I don't know. Guess she had a stroke. Nobody told me, goddammit. And here I been plannin' a present for that lady for eight goddamn years. Wanted to thank her for all she done for me, y'know."

"Yeah, right. Good thing she passed away," Ron said with a chuckle. "Likely you wouldn't be here today. They'd find her all beat up and have you back in the slammer."

"Yeah, but, man, it would be worth it. It would be so *goddamn* worth it." Bobby slammed his right fist on the sofa cushion.

Kenny felt a chill despite the hot room. He did not want to hear this. All he ever knew was that Rita was the woman who had refused to let Bobby stay at her place after his escape from a minimum security prison outside Milwaukee. Of course, if she hadn't called the cops on him, she would have gone to jail herself. But what Kenny didn't know and didn't want to know was the rest of the story.

———

He could recall only that there had been a child, Rita's child by another man. A girl. Deer hunters had found the little body frozen, the collarbone fractured and evidence of other bruises on the arms and legs. The kid had run from her mother's house in the dead of winter. No jacket even.

Bobby's defense lawyer had alleged his client was framed by the former girlfriend, that Rita was an abusive parent, and managed to get him a reduced sentence on a charge of battery to a child, but people who knew Bobby knew better. They knew.

After all, Bobby Schradtke was a habitual offender going back to his early teens. He had launched his career by running away to join a carnival, but he was soon arrested for robbery and sent home. This sparked years of arrests for theft, possession of burglary tools, stealing cars, and two episodes of attempted sexual assault on a minor. It was an arrest for distributing crack cocaine on tribal lands that won him his most recent sentence—eight years and four months. But now, in his early forties, Bobby was a free man.

———

"So this town's gone soft," Bobby was saying. "Hell, that's good for my business."

"What do you mean?" said Kenny. "Hard as hell to make a living up here still. Been this way for years."

"Can't believe you got a broad as chief of police. Now that's what I call sweet. Sweet and easy."

"What exactly did you hear?" Ron asked, blowing cigarette smoke towards an open window. "That lady's been around a couple years now. She's tough. I seen her kneecap a couple drunks my size. I would not call her 'sweet.'"

"Had a meeting this morning with my parole officer and she was there. Kept quiet. Didn't say much. A couple other guys got paroled were there, too, so we were about six of us altogether. We got the rules read, the usual shit," said Bobby with a shrug of indifference.

"The way I see it," said Bobby, spreading his hands as if he had a map laid out in front of him, "Loon Lake's got a female cop and that by my standards makes for easy pickings." A spider laugh. "Ron, you and me, we got work to do. I'll show you how to double the dough you've been making breaking your butt with all that logging—"

Kenny felt an urgent need to leave the room. Leave now or you're an accomplice, he told himself.

"Speaking of logging," said Ron, straightening up in his chair and motioning with his hand for Kenny to join the conversation, "Kenny and I got a ... *dilemma* ... we'd like to discuss with you. Gotta problem with this joker by the name of Calverson ..."

"Yeah? Hold that thought—gotta see a man about a horse," said Bobby, getting to his feet. Ron had relaxed into the chair next to Kenny with his legs stretched out and his ankles crossed. As Bobby walked by, he gave his brother's feet a swift kick with the toe of one pointed cowboy boot.

Kenny could see from Ron's face that the kick both hurt and embarrassed him in front of Kenny. Ron squinted as he rubbed an ankle. He stared at the bathroom door until it closed, then said in voice that sounded like a curse: "Welcome home, big brother."

———

Minutes later, with Bobby back on the sofa twisting the cap off another beer, Ron recounted their morning confrontation with Curt Calverson. "So?" Bobby rolled a toothpick across his lips as he mulled over Ron's story. "Whaddya want exactly—the money? Or hurt the guy?"

"Both," said Ron.

"Just the money," said Kenny. "No trouble."

"Ah," said Bobby, "no trouble, no fun."

Kenny shook his head and said, "Count me out, you two. All I want is to get paid for the work I did. I'll take fifty cents on the buck."

Bobby laughed, "No, you won't. You'll get a hundred percent of what you're owed. Leave it to me. Now I'll tell you what, you two. Give me a couple a days. Gotta check in with some guys I know. Kenny, don't you worry." Bobby shook an index finger at him. "I did eight years and don't plan to do a day more. You're talkin' to a smart guy."

"Just keep me out of it if you got trouble in mind," said Kenny, repeating himself as he got to his feet. "Gotta go, fellas, got dogs to feed."

# CHAPTER 10

Osborne pulled to the curb behind the police cruiser parked in front of the Nystrom Antiques Emporium. A "Closed" sign hung at an angle on the front door, which was locked. Osborne rapped twice but no one came. He peered past the sign, but the interior of the shop was in shadow.

Remembering that Bart's office was in the back, he hurried down the sidewalk that ran along the side of the building towards a back entrance. That door was open. Without knocking, he stepped inside what must have been a back porch before the house was converted to a store. Now it was a storeroom for cleaning supplies. A door at the top of a short stairway opened into a small kitchen that held a coffee machine and an old refrigerator. "He-l-l-o-o, Chief Ferris? Bart?" said Osborne in a loud voice.

No answer. He walked through the kitchen to the shop's interior. Off to the right was a hallway at the end of which he could see Bart's office. The lights were on in the office but the room was empty.

It dawned on Osborne they must be in the basement. Turning around, he walked back down the hall and into the darkened shop. The door to the basement stairs stood open and beyond it he could see light. "Chief Ferris? Bart?" Just as he called out, Lew dashed up the basement stairs.

"Doc, thanks goodness you're here. Boy, do I need your help this afternoon. Pecore was called down to Madison this morning. They're re-opening a rape case from 1988 for DNA testing, and he had to drive the evidence boxes down.

"Let me re-phrase that—the idiot isn't sure which is the right box, so he's taking everything he's got from 1988 and hoping the crime lab officials don't notice how he's compromised the integrity of the Loon Lake Police Department with his lousy attention to the chain of custody. If I'm lucky, they won't be fooled and he'll be suspended for—"

Lew's face was flushed, her eyes sparking with frustration as she rushed her words. Under normal circumstances, Osborne would have relished the moment: every time he saw her coming towards him, it felt like the first time. The lively face, nut brown from the sun under a cap of short dark curls, the eyes frank, the mouth quick to smile. And the body—she wasn't a small woman, but broad-shouldered and slightly wide in the hip with a frame that was strong and fit. Yet sturdy as Lewellyn Ferris might appear, she had a body that could curve soft as a whisper into his.

But these were not normal circumstances and all he could see beyond his worry was hope that Lew could help him help Mason.

He felt himself listening from a distance as Lew said, "—I've got another meeting at three and I'm trying like the dickens to get out of the office by four-thirty so I have time to shower and change before catching up with the reunion crowd. But, Doc, what you found here is disturbing. And you're right—we have a victim, not some museum piece.

"Did you notice the tag on that rug said it came from the Bobcat Inn?"

Lew's eyes widened with excitement and she spoke so fast Osborne couldn't get a word in. "That was old Abner Conjurski's place. He disappeared long before I joined the force, but I've seen the file. The Loon Lake police never did know what happened."

Planting both hands on her hips, Lew said, "I have to wonder if those aren't poor old Abner's remains down there. Y'know? So, Doc, I'll call the Wausau Crime Lab and let them know it's not an emergency but we need their help as soon as they can work us in. Meanwhile, I'm deputizing you to secure the scene better than what we've got right now and arrange to meet—"

"No." Osborne put up a hand to stop her. "No, Lewellyn. I … I can't do that."

Lew paused, her mouth open in surprise. Her eyes searched his face, "What's wrong? Oh … Doc, you look like someone died. What is it—are you alright?" She held her breath and reached out to take his arm as if expecting to hear the worst.

Osborne couldn't speak. He shook his head and tried to get a few words out but all he could manage was a choked, "Um, Mason. I think she may have been …" His voice was a whisper as he managed to say, "… molested. This morning."

"Oh-h, no," said Lew, exhaling the words. The distress that flooded her face he hoped never to see again in his lifetime. "Is she hurt?"

"I—I, that's what—I don't know. That's why … Lew, I need your help." He could feel his eyes brimming.

"Bart!" Lew turned to shout down the stairwell. "I have an emergency. I'm taking over your office. Door closed. Not sure how long." She grabbed Osborne's left hand and pulled him back through the shop to the small office where she closed the door, pulled two chairs together and motioned for him to sit.

"Wait," she held up one hand as he started to speak and reached for the cell phone she wore in a holster next to the .9mm Sig Sauer. "Marlene, cancel that three o'clock appointment I have, would you, please? It's another one of those probation reviews, and they'll have to reschedule. Tell them I have a felony assault to deal with and I'll be in touch when I can."

Lew tucked the phone away, turned her chair so she was facing Osborne, took both his hands in hers and eyes fixed on his said, "Tell me what you know. Take your time. First, though, where's Mason now?"

"She's home, she seems okay but she won't tell us—"

"I'm not surprised. Children often have a hard time telling what happened when they've been badly frightened."

"That's what Mallory said—"

"Start at the beginning, Doc ..."

———•———

"We have twenty-three registered sex offenders in and around
Loon Lake," Lew said when he had finished sharing every
detail that he knew or suspected since talking to C.J. Calverson and spotting Bobby Schradtke's car. "I can have a status
report run on where each of those individuals were this morning. They are required by law to keep us informed of their
whereabouts at all times."

"Twenty-three! I had no idea. Do you regularly alert people to these offenders?"

"We try to keep parents aware, but sex offenders are under
the sheriff's jurisdiction, not the police department's. We have
to follow their lead. Now tell me who this C.J. person is."

"She's new to Loon Lake—young, maybe in her twen-
ties—and recently married to an older guy named Curt Calverson. I've never met the man. Erin seemed to know who he is.
They bought that big house kiddie corner from Court House
and they have a lake home on Big Moccasin. Once she calmed
Mason down, Mason seemed to trust her. She offered to take
myself and Mason out fishing on their pontoon this afternoon.
She and I and Erin—we were thinking that if we could get her
mind off things for a while that she might open up.

"Now, Lew, I haven't said a word to Erin about my concern that Mason may have been molested. Didn't occur to me
until I happened to drive by Edna Schradtke's place and saw

that old car that belongs to her son, Bobby. That worthless
piece of shit is back in town and, Lew, that creep tried to pull
Mallory into his car one day when she was just a kid. She
wouldn't tell us what happened that night. I didn't know the
truth until after Mary Lee died.

"I can't tell you how bad I feel that she couldn't trust us.
Could Mason be shutting down for the same reason? Am I
crazy to think this way?"

Lew reached for both his hands and grasped them firmly
between hers as she said, "Look, it won't be easy if she has been
hurt. I may need to bring in a professional therapist but, please,
Doc, know that between you and me and her parents, we'll get
Mason all the help she needs to determine what, if anything,
has happened to her. Until then, let's hope for the best."

She stood up and pulled Osborne into her arms for a long,
comforting hug. "And if she has been hurt, we can help with
that, too. You'd be amazed at how resilient kids are. Keep in
mind that one out of four kids experience some kind of sexual
abuse as they're growing up. The good news is that today we
have professionals trained to help them cope with the trauma."

"I sure hope so," said Osborne, feeling a slight sense of relief. "You know," he said taking a deep breath, "now that you
mention it, there was an incident back when I was in boarding school. I think I told you I was six when my father sent me
off to the Jesuits. When I was in the fourth grade, a number
of the boys in my dorm were being victimized by an older
boy from the high school—until one of the young ones finally
went to the priest in charge of our dorm. The older boy was
gone the next day."

"Really," said Lew. "Wouldn't it be nice to know what gave the younger boy the courage to speak up? "

"I may be able to find out. The boy who blew the whistle and I have stayed in touch over the years. He's a retired MD living in Indiana. I could call him and see if he remembers the incident and if he minds telling me why he did what he did."

"Worth a try, Doc. Look, I'll cancel my evening so I can help you with this," said Lew, setting the chairs back where they'd been.

"Absolutely not. I'll give my old friend a call and see what I can find out."

"I think it might be a good idea, if you're able to reach him—and before you see Mason—that you and I talk. Have Marlene patch you through to me. And, Doc, this comes before any silly party."

Before they left the room, Lew reached to pull him close again. "Dr. Osborne," she whispered, "Mason has all the right people around her. We'll make this okay."

"I hope you're right," said Osborne. "I'll never forgive myself if she's a victim of the same creep that went after Mallory. I can't let that happen again."

"Doc," said Lew, her voice firm, "I want you to get over that thought. Whoever it was this morning—it was not Bobby Schradtke. He was in a meeting with his probation officer, myself, the sheriff and three other parolees. Three hours. It could not possibly have been Bobby."

"That's good to know," said Osborne. He stopped at the entrance to the kitchen and turned. "Lew, I feel bad I can't help you out here."

"Please, don't even think about it. I'll work something out. I'll call the Wausau boys right now. They owe me one anyway. We've got a victim who isn't going anywhere—that much we know. The main issue is getting the rug and the remains out of here so Bart can re-open his store."

CHAPTER 11

Throughout the drive home Osborne could not stop worry-
ing: did he have a current phone number for Pete Murphy?
After all, it had been five years since they had caught up with
each other during the academy's centennial celebration.

After arriving home and checking on Mike, who was intent
on stalking a squirrel and could care less if his water dish was full,
Osborne sat down at the desk in his den, opened his address
book and picked up the phone.

To his relief, a familiar voice answered on the second ring.
"Paul, hey! Good to hear from you—what's up?" asked Pete. "Finally coming through with an invitation to fish that beautiful
lake of yours, are you?"

"We can sure discuss that," said Osborne, "but, Pete, the fact
is I've got a difficult situation with one of my grandchildren, and
my hunch is you may be able to help me out a little here. Do you
have time to talk for a few minutes?"

"I've got the time, not sure I've got any answers. Remember,
Paul, I was a GP and not a pediatrician—"

"This has nothing to do with medicine."

"Really? Well, you've piqued my curiosity, old friend. I'll do my best to help you out. But give me a clue, won't you?" Pete sounded so relaxed and happy that Osborne wondered if he was right to ask questions that could bring back unpleasant memories.

"This is about an incident when you and I were in grade school, Pete. I've never forgotten that you were the guy who blew the whistle on that Collins kid. Remember that bully?"

"Never forget him. Wonder whatever happened to that jerk."

"You were the only one on your floor with the guts to say anything even though a number of the other boys knew he was hurting those kids. Everyone was too scared to say anything. I guess ..." Osborne paused, uncertain how to ask the next question.

"My question is—would you mind talking about that, Pete? I would like to know what gave *you* the confidence to tell Father Kucera what was happening."

"And why is that, Paul? You have a grandchild who is being bullied?"

"Possibly ... maybe worse ..."

"I see. Well, if it helps I'm happy to tell you why I did what I did. And you may find it rather ironic that it all started with one of *my* grandparents—my grandmother ..."

———◦•———

Twenty minutes later Osborne had a plan. He called Erin. "Is Mason still up to go fishing?" He knew the answer before he asked, of course, and chuckled at the whoop of joy he heard in the background. "Good, I'll be there by three-thirty."

Opening the back of the Subaru, he carefully laid two metal tubes side by side—the beige one held his old Sage fly rod and the forest green tube with the shiny brass cap held the new Winston fly rod that Lew and his daughters had given him for his birthday. He double-checked his fishing duffle to be sure it held a couple extra reels and, finally, he folded his fly fishing vest so that the pockets bulging with boxes of trout flies wouldn't get crushed by Mike's car kennel. At the last minute, he threw in an extra fishing hat—the one that was too small for him.

Before leaving the house, he let the dog out of the yard and together they headed for the water: Osborne took the stairs while Mike leaped ahead, dashing onto the dock before coming to a skidding halt at the end. Much as the black lab loved to swim, he refused to dive.

Osborne ambled out over the water to stand beside the dog and speculate. It was a favorite pastime of his, and Mason had asked him once why he spent so much time alone on his dock. "I like to speculate," he had said and left to her to fig-ure what he meant.

A cerulean sky had cast its spell across the water with only the distant horizon of dark firs to separate the matching blues. The water surface was still. Not a cloud marred the sky, not a sound the air. Not even the hum of a distant outboard motor could be heard. Peace reigned. Osborne raised his face to the sun, *speculating.*

Summer afternoon in June: life should be perfect. Old bones should not tumble out of rugs; little girls should not be terrified. How would this day end?

He found his favorite perch on the bench anchoring the end of the dock and took the time to say—as was his habit when life pressed hard—a *Hail Mary*. A short prayer, it had been his favorite since childhood, since those days with the Jesuits: a wistful attempt to ensure he was doing the right thing.

After three *Hail Marys*, he and the dog sat very still, listening as a trio of breezes came rippling across the water, whispering their secrets to the tall pines guarding the shore.

Secrets, Osborne thought, goddamn secrets. I've had it with secrets. He reached to rub the black lab behind his ears then gave him a swift pat, "Okay, guy, gotta go. Wish me luck."

And Mike leaped up to do as he was asked with a wag of his tail and a wide, toothy smile.

———•◦•———

As he drove into town, left hand on the steering wheel, right hand clutching the cell phone, he was able to reach Marlene on the switchboard and ask to be patched through to Lew. It took just a minute to relay the gist of Pete's story and let her know what he was planning to do.

"Well," she said after a brief pause, "can't hurt to give it a try, Doc. Mason's got an aggressive side to her and this may just hit her right. But, please, call me later. Even if it's after five, I'll have my phone with me and I'm going to worry until we know more."

CHAPTER 12

Hunched forward in anticipation, Mason was perched on the porch steps, a blue and white-striped beach towel draped across her shoulders and a bright red life jacket clutched to her chest.

"Grandpa!" She waved as she jumped to her feet and danced down the stairs towards Osborne's car. Shouting as she ran, she said, "C.J. invited us to a picnic, too! Root beer, bratwurst. Even Ray is coming." She yanked open the car door and thrust her head inside. "And it's just me who gets to go with you, Grandpa. Not Cody."

Osborne turned away to smile. He was not surprised to hear that excluding her little brother would make the afternoon even more special. As Mason clambered into the front seat, her mother appeared in the doorway, a blue backpack in her hands. She held it high as she said, "Dad, got a minute?"

"Be right there," said Osborne, holding the car door open until he was sure Mason had fastened her seat belt.

"Here," said Erin, as he reached the porch, "a change of clothes in case you-know-who falls in, which I can guarantee she will. And jeans and a sweatshirt for when it's cool later. She's got her swimsuit on under her shorts and T-shirt."

"Has she said anything more about this morning?" asked Osborne, reaching for the backpack.

"Not a word, but she is certainly thrilled to be going off with you and her new best friend," said Erin. "By the way, C.J. had me call Ray to be sure he knew he was invited." Erin grimaced, "He's coming all right, Dad, he's bringing a '... surprise.'" Erin mimicked Ray's deliberate delay when imparting critical information.

"Jeez Louise," said Osborne with a wry smile as he gave his daughter a quick peck on the cheek, "I'm not sure how many more surprises this old man can manage."

---

On pulling to a stop in a parking space below the deck fronting the Calverson's lake house, Osborne had spotted a handwritten sign directing them to take a side path between a garden and the south side of the house. "Mason, you run on ahead," he said to the child, who needed no urging—as she was already flying down the path. "I'll be right behind you."

He gathered up the fly rods and fishing gear and slung Mason's backpack over one shoulder. Rounding the back of the house, he found himself at the top of a steep hill and a stone walkway that led, in a series of switchbacks, down to the water.

Pausing to look below, he could see the back of a woman in a white T-shirt and navy blue shorts, most likely C.J., loading coolers from the dock onto the pontoon. The pontoon, which was one of the largest ones that Osborne had ever seen, was tethered to one of two docks fronting a wide, wooden deck. Alongside the other dock was a covered shore station, which held a speedboat and two jet skis.

As he started down the stone pathway, he was a good fifty yards behind Mason who was bouncing her way down and shouting loud enough for the entire shoreline to hear. Mason's cheerful calls alerted C.J., who glanced up with a pleased smile—a smile that broke into an even wider grin when she saw Osborne.

"Hey, folks, you're just in time for the picnic cruise. All aboard," she said, wiping her hands on her shorts. "C'mon, I'm almost ready. Dr. Osborne, feel free to use the boathouse if you need to change—there's a shower and everything in there." She pointed to a boathouse off one side of the deck that had been obscured by trees when Osborne was looking down from the top of the hill.

Osborne deposited Mason's backpack and his fishing equipment on the dock, then straightened up and, hands on his hips, said, "C.J., if you're up for it, I thought I would give you and Mason a lesson on fly fishing while we're on the water this afternoon. Big Moccasin is known for its bluegills— I'm assuming, of course, that you two wouldn't mind learning how to cast a fly rod …"

"Serious?" asked C.J., moving forward to help Osborne load all the gear onto the pontoon. It wasn't until she moved that Osborne could see there was another person on board.

Seated to one side at the rear of the pontoon and nearly hidden under the boat awning was an older man whom Osborne figured to be in his mid to late fifties.

"Did you hear that, Curt?" said C.J. calling back over her shoulder. "Dr. Osborne is going to teach me how to cast with a fly rod." The man, who was sitting with his elbows on his knees and head down, was talking into a cell phone. At the sound of his wife's voice, without raising his head he gave a preoccupied wave.

"I was worried about having room to practice some roll casts," Osborne said, stepping onto the pontoon and looking around, "but this is a good-sized boat—plenty of space. By the way, C.J., I forgot one thing in my car and it's rather heavy. Would you mind giving me a hand?" He pointed up towards the house on the hill. C.J. caught the look in his eye and nodded.

"Mason," she said, pointing to an open cooler, "I'm putting you in charge of the sodas. Would you finish burying those cans in the ice, please?" As the youngster knelt to follow orders, C.J. smiled at Osborne and hurried to follow him up the stone walkway towards the house.

Midway up, Osborne paused in the center of one of the switchbacks where he could keep an eye on Mason as they talked. "I have a plan," he said to C.J., "that I've talked over with Chief Ferris, who has a lot more experience with these matters than I do. She seems to think it might help us get Mason to open up."

"That would be a relief," said C.J., "I'm so worried that someone was lurking around our place in town and that's who frightened your granddaughter."

After a quick explanation of what he was planning to do and why, Osborne said, "... so after we've been casting for a while, I'm hoping there is a way that I might find some time to chat with Mason in private. She'll be feeling good about herself, she'll feel safe and I have to believe she trusts me enough to tell me what it was that upset her so."

"Well," said C.J., "let's hope you're right. I know what I can do to make it easy for you two to have some time together and it fits with just how I like to picnic on the lake. After we've fished for awhile, we'll anchor by that island out there."

She pointed across the lake. "It has a nice sandy beach that makes it easy to pull up near shore and wade in. With help from my husband and your friend, Ray, we'll get a grill going on the beach while you and Mason talk. What do you think—would half an hour give you enough time?"

"I would think so," said Osborne. "I hope you don't mind my forcing a casting lesson on you but it's something Mason has been bugging me to teach her—"

"Are you kidding? It's been on my list of things to do ever since I knew we were moving here. I'm delighted, Dr. Osborne."

But not as delighted as she was a second later when she looked past Osborne, who stood facing her, to see another figure descending the stairs. "Ray, you made it!" said C.J. as she ran forward.

Remembering that Ray had promised to bring a "surprise," Osborne felt a moment's trepidation. Before turning around, he prayed that the surprise would have a full set of teeth.

CHAPTER **13**

The lanky kid shadowing Ray had to be two inches taller than when Osborne had last seen him. Taller and tidier. Gone were the eyebrow piercing, the nose piercing, the lip piercing and the black T-shirt: all that remained of Nick's previous fashion statements were four silver studs along the lobe of his right ear.

"Hey, you razzbonya," said Osborne, rushing forward to take the boy by the shoulders and give him a friendly shake. "Ray didn't say you were in town. Here for the rest of the summer?"

"I wish," said Nick, grinning as he reached to give Osborne's hand a firm shake. Though his face had filled out since they last met, there would never be any mistaking that Nick was the son of the dark beauty with an arctic heart who had tried to convince Ray that she had borne his child.

"Doc," said Ray, "Nick surprised me, too. Showed up at my place about an hour ago to tell me he's pre-fishing the Moccasin chain with a team from the University of Wisconsin-Madison. They've qualified for the finals in the National Collegiate Bass Fishing Tournament, which starts next week, so I thought it might help if I show him some of my honey holes."

"Help? Hell! How 'bout a *guarantee*," said Osborne, turning back to the boy. "So when did you get into bass fishing, Nick? I thought Ray had convinced you that walleye fishing is the way to go."

Nick shrugged. It was long-standing argument among Osborne's buddies over their morning McDonald's coffee: walleye fishermen like to consider themselves more skilled than bass fishermen—insisting that walleyes are smarter, wilier than bass. Bass fishermen swear the opposite.

"Yeah, Ray gave me some trouble about this, but for fourteen thousand bucks I'll fish carp if I have to."

"Whoa, the purse is that good?" Osborne asked. "I had no idea."

"Oh yeah, the college tournaments are really popular, Doc. Our team's been fishing since June and done okay—got five largemouths weighing just over thirteen and a third pounds in the semis."

"Wow." Osborne was impressed.

"Thanks to my good buddy here, I've got some decent skills," said Nick with an appreciative nod towards Ray.

"Ray suckered you in." Osborne gave him a light punch in the shoulder. "He let you think you hooked those fish but, fact is, son, the fish hooked you. Right?"

"Absolutely," said Nick. He thrust his hands in the pockets of his khaki shorts as he said with a sheepish expression: "I am thinking of doing this for a living ..."

"Not the easiest way to get rich," said Ray. "I'm proof of that."

"Rich is relative," said Nick. "Thing about you is you're fun to be around, man—you're a happy guy. More'n I can say for my stepfather, who's worth a few million and can't start the day without a shot of Jack Daniels." Nick raised his eyebrows, "He says it beats Zoloft."

"Hey, enough talk, you guys," said C.J., "let's get this show on the road." And she waved for them to follow her back down to the dock. Ray tipped his head towards C.J. as he caught Nick's eye with a wink.

Yep, thought Osborne, some things never change: Ray would always love fishing and he would always love pretty women, and one or both could always get him into trouble.

———◦◦◦———

Ambling down the walkway behind Nick and Ray, Osborne reflected on what had been a tense summer two years ago: three long months when Ray had tried to be the dad he thought he was to a recalcitrant teenager from New York City. It took a series of life-threatening events crossed with the lure of the northwoods to weaken Nick's resistance to authority—not to mention his addiction to the Internet.

But nature worked its magic on the kid—fueling a love for the mournful wail of the loon, the heavy breathing of the wind through the pines, the soothing lap of waves in the dark. Ray, in turn, found himself charmed by a boy whose curiosity and willingness to take chances rivaled his own.

Thus was born a kinship that had to survive devastating news when a DNA test (requested by someone other than

Ray) delivered one simple, heartbreaking fact: Nick's mother had lied. Ray was not the boy's biological father.

No matter. Ray had no intention of letting go: "Nick," he'd said, chin thrust forward, "I may not have been there when you were born, but … you are my son."

———◆———

Oblivious to his guests, Curt had remained engrossed in his cell phone conversation while his wife untied the pontoon from its mooring. When her husband still didn't move to take his place running the boat, C.J. had shrugged and anointed Ray skipper.

"It's up to you or we'll be stuck here forever," she'd said, beckoning Ray forward.

So Ray had taken over the captain's chair while Nick settled into the seat beside him. As they crossed the lake, C.J. was standing, legs apart and knees bent for balance, behind Ray and Nick, leaning over their shoulders with a wide smile on her face as the three shouted back and forth over the roar of outboard.

Osborne sat with one arm encircling Mason's shoulders as they sat side by side on one of the pontoon's padded benches. He gazed across Big Moccasin while the pontoon scooted over the waves towards the western shore. The late afternoon sun was glorious on the water: electric blue and sparkling.

CHAPTER 14

As the boat picked up speed, Mason snuggled closer, glancing up every few minutes with a happy grin. Clutched tight in her right hand was the new Scientific Angler reel he had handed to her for safekeeping as they left the dock. Between his feet Osborne cradled two long metal cases holding his fly rods.

It was a good ten minutes before the boat slowed and Ray shifted down to a slow trolling speed. "Doc," he said, "I'm going to run us along the shoreline here for a bit. Point out the key spots for Nick to lock into his GPS. No problem for us if you want Mason and C.J. casting off the sides. You won't be in our way." Nodding towards Curt, he rolled his eyes. The man was still on the phone.

"Okay," said Osborne, getting to his feet. The late day thermals off the potato fields had died, leaving the lake still as glass. Only the burbling of the pontoon's trolling motor disturbed the surface.

"Mason and C.J.," said Osborne, uncapping his rod cases, "I'd like both of you up front here." He pointed out two spots, one on each side of the pontoon. Mason and C.J. took their places. Moments later, fly rods rigged and eyes bright with anticipation, they stood ready for action.

"Watch closely now," said Osborne, reaching for the Winston rod that Mason was holding, "I'm going to demonstrate. First thing you need to know is that casting a fly rod is easy— all it takes is a little coaching. And, ladies, women tend to be very good at it because—unlike spin casting—it requires no muscle."

As he talked, he brought his elbow up and down for a perfect roll cast. Possibly the best he'd ever done. Damn, he thought, why wasn't Lew here to see this? Oh well.

"In fact, the more muscle used, the worse the cast. It's all in the timing—" Again the elbow was up and down and his fly line flew forward straight and smooth to land light as a dragonfly on the water.

"So today you'll learn the roll cast, which is the best for catching bluegills off a pontoon like this. Watch me a few more times—then I'll have you try ..." Again the elbow up, down and the thumb snapping forward.

"See how I keep my hand, forearm and upper arm in line? Watch my wrist: I start by bending it down so I can feel the rod against my arm here—" He held his arm out so they could both see, "now I take my wrist straight back, lift ... and lower my elbow as I *push* with my thumb to let the fly line out—that's the power snap that Lewellyn Ferris taught me. She learned it from Joan Wulff, who was a world champion fly fisherman."

He demonstrated twice more, then handed the rod to Mason. "C.J., Mason, you try it."

"This doesn't look like the movies," said C.J. after a few tries. "I want to look like Brad Pitt in *A River Runs Through It*."

Osborne chuckled. "Hold your horses, C.J. Next trip, I promise you'll learn how to backcast—but not today or we'll hook your husband in the head. One step at a time, kiddo."

"Oh?" said C.J. with a tease in her voice. "Do you mean we might have to do this again pretty soon?" The prospect appeared to please her and Osborne suspected it had less to do with backcasting than spending more time with a certain fellow who did not have a cell phone permanently attached to his ear.

She raised the Sage rod, bringing her arm back and sideways as if to throw a baseball. "No—no swinging," said Osborne, straightening her arm. "Bring the rod *straight* up. Bring your thumbnail to your forehead with your hand close to your face ... lead with your elbow, finish with your hand forward ... good! Okay, again. Keep in mind that the rod is an *extension* of your arm."

Mason and C.J. cast again and again, eager to get it right. Osborne watched, then offered the tips he heard so often from Lew: "Use your thumb to target an area ... okay, lead with your elbow and if the line coils try again ... keep going 'til you get a nice, straight cast. If it coils, you chopped too low and didn't push out ... think of *punching* your thumb forward."

"So if I do this right, I'll catch a fish?" asked Mason, raising her elbow and nearly clocking herself in the forehead, she was so determined.

"Well, that's part of it," said Osborne. "I still have to teach you how to pick the right trout fly—the one that looks just like the insects the fish are eating—how to 'match the hatch' as they say."

Mason looked at him in surprise: "They don't eat worms?"

"They do. Yes, they do. But that's a political issue we'll discuss another day. For now keep practicing—you're getting it."

As Osborne settled back to watch, he let his mind drift to an evening of fly fishing weeks earlier. The kind of evening that always settled his soul …

———·———

Lew had managed to escape her office early and they'd sped north to a place known only to a few lucky anglers as "secret lake." And a secret it was: well hidden with no motorboats allowed, only a few cabins to mar the shoreline and a bounty of seldom-harvested rainbow trout.

They had hiked in a mile and a half then sat on boulders to pull on their waders. Osborne had entered the water behind Lew, following her lead from a distance. By the time she reached the spot she wanted, the sun had dipped below the spires of the balsams lining the western shore.

He took care to stay far enough behind that he wouldn't disturb the fish Lew was targeting—but he wanted to be close enough to watch as she fished. A rank beginner still, he knew he could learn more from watching than struggling with his own floppy fly line.

And so he watched as Lew waded in until she was waist deep in the darkening, silent water. Random lights glowed gold along the far shore, a fish slurped. She began to rock back and forth, her body supple as a dancer's, moving with the grace of a doe. A whisper as the fly line unfurled behind her only to shoot forward with the momentum of a power snap that sent the line straight and true, dropping a #12 Adams dry fly with such stealth that the trout leaping for a fluttering insect was stunned.

"Doc," said C.J., interrupting his reverie, "my arm is tired. Do you mind if I sit for a while?"

"Of course not. We're here to have fun." Osborne took the fly rod from her hands and set it nearby as C.J. sauntered across the deck to plunk herself down by Ray and Nick.

"So, Ray," said C.J., wrapping her arms around her knees as she spoke, "how come you do all this fishing instead of making a living like an honest man?"

Osborne resisted a chuckle: now how many people had he heard ask that identical question of his subsistence level trailer home-living neighbor? Some asked it to his face, others behind his back.

"Well," said Ray, lifting his eyebrows as he looked at his questioner, "I figured out early in life that ... fishing ... is the most fun you can have ... with your clothes on." Nick turned his head away so C.J. couldn't see the look on his face.

"No, I'm serious," said C.J., lowering her voice. She glanced towards the rear of the pontoon where her husband sat with his back to them, still anchored to his cell phone.

"Serious? You want *serious*," said Ray.

"He doesn't do serious," said Nick.

"Yeah. I do," said C. J, ignoring Nick's remark. She crossed her arms and waited.

Ray dropped his head and studied his feet as if the answer was in his flip flops, then looked up, "I tried a year in college as a business major because my folks said it was the only way I'd ever find out how to make money—but nothing about helping American businesses become more efficient made me want to get up in the morning … so I quit."

"What *does* make you want to get up in the morning?"

"Fishing. Simple as that. Not a lot of money, but plenty of fresh air." The three of them sat in silence for a few moments pondering Ray's answer. Then Ray said, "what about you, C.J.? What makes *you* want to get up in the morning?"

The girl stared at him, her eyes widening. To his surprise, Osborne could see tears brimming as she opened her mouth.

"Grandpa!" shouted Mason with a sudden lurch backwards, the Winston rod bent towards the water. "I think I got a fish!"

Jumping to his feet, Ray rushed forward. "Set the hook! Set the hook!" he cried. "Mason, keep that rod tip high!"

Osborne stayed back. He knew from experience not to interfere. A fish on the line is guaranteed to turn Ray Pradt into a kid again. "That's it," said Ray, voice high with excite-

ment, "bring him alongside ... careful ... careful. Watch that
rod tip!"

"What is it? A muskie?" said C.J., crowding in behind Ray.
"Is it a big fish?"

"Sure is," said Ray, reaching down to grab the fly line and
pull up a wriggling seven-inch blue gill. "Where's the camera?
Doc, you got a camera?"

"Here," said Nick, thrusting a disposable camera into Osborne's hand as Ray slipped the barbless hook from the
bluegill.

"Hold it gently like this," Ray said, guiding Mason's hands
into a cradle that wouldn't harm the fish. "We're catch-and-
release today, hon. Let Grandpa take your picture and then
this guy gets to go home. Okay?"

Mason nodded as happily as if she'd caught a six-foot tar-
pon—smiling for the camera, hands gentle on the bluegill.
Then she got down on her knees and stretched along the
deck, arms over the side of the pontoon so the little fish could
swim away. She scrambled to her feet, fists clenched as she
jumped up and down saying, "Oh, Grandpa, wait'll Cody
hears this!"

"Your first fish with a fly rod—wow!!" said Ray, whacking
her on the back so hard she nearly went flying off the boat
after her catch.

"What the hell is all the noise?" said Curt, marching forward from the back of the boat and covering the mouthpiece
of his cell phone.

"Mason caught a bluegill on a fly rod," said C.J.

"Oh for Christ's sake, keep it down, will you?" said Curt. "I can't hear a goddamn word—" He turned back towards the rear of the boat.

"What's he doing that's so important?" Ray asked. "Does he ever take a break?"

"Moving money," said C.J. with a tight smile, "he's always *moving money*."

Curt must have heard her because he said something into the phone and flipped it shut. He turned back to walk over to where C.J. was standing.

"What?" she said, looking at him just as, palm open, he slammed his right hand across her face so hard she staggered back against the railing.

"How many times have I told you—*never talk about my business*." Curt loomed over her as she fell to her knees gasping for breath through harsh sobs.

"Hey!" said Ray, grabbing Curt by the arm. "You don't treat women that way—not on my watch, you don't."

"Then you won't be back," said Curt, yanking his arm away.

Osborne pulled Mason towards him. The pontoon was nearing the cove on the small island. C.J. wiped at her face as Curt headed to the back of the boat, where he sat back down.

"I'm okay," said C.J., pushing Ray and Nick away as they reached to help her stand up. "No, please, this is so embarrassing." She gave a weak grin. "Let's have our picnic, all right?"

"We can do that," said Ray, patting her shoulder. He shot a glance at Osborne, and he wasn't smiling.

CHAPTER 15

It was a subdued party of five that let themselves down, one by one, into knee-deep water to wade up to the sandy beach where C.J. planned to have the picnic. Taking whispered directions from their hostess, Nick and Ray carried ashore the grill and two large picnic baskets. Osborne handed a six-pack of Sprecher's Root Beer to Mason, then grabbed four lightweight folding chairs and a quilt, which he tucked under one arm.

"What else can I do?" he said after setting everything down on the sand near C.J.

"We'll take it from here, Dr. Osborne," said C.J., straightening up and dusting off her hands. "I have an idea—why don't you and Mason check out the other side of the island? See if there's a better spot for our picnic." She winked.

Osborne squeezed her arm in appreciation and said, "Have you noticed most people around here call me 'Doc?' Why don't you do the same? Drop the *Doctor*," he said, dropping his voice to the low tone he once saved for flossing instructions. "Doctor sounds way too serious for an old retired guy who spends most of his day in a fishing boat. You are a friend, C.J., not a patient."

"Thank you," said C.J. She gave him a sheepish smile as if she knew he was just trying to make her feel better. She glanced back at the pontoon where Curt reclined on one of the padded benches: arms folded, feet propped up on a railing and a khaki fishing hat covering his eyes. He appeared to be sound asleep.

"I don't know what to do ..." She pursed her lips as if holding back another flood of emotion. "And I am *so* embarrassed."

"Let it go," said Osborne. "We've all been there. Right now you've got your hands full with those two—better keep an eye on them or you'll be embarrassed in ways you never expected." He pointed towards Ray and Nick who were wrestling with the portable grill. C.J. grinned, "I'll bet you're right."

Turning towards the lake, Osborne shouted, "Hey, young lady," in an alert to Mason who had waded back into the water chasing frogs, "time for you and me to take a walk. Go exploring."

"O-o-o-KAY!" shouted Mason as she splashed his way. Her eyes had been tinged with worry ever since the altercation on the pontoon but the invitation to walk with her grandfather appeared to spark glee and relief.

They trudged along a sandy, pebble-strewn path for a few yards. It led up a steep hill and down the other side with enough tall grasses and tag alder shrubs to hide them from the others. A rotting tree trunk lying lengthwise beckoned, and Osborne sank down with a sigh.

Mason plopped down alongside, hands tucked between her knees and a serious look on her face. Osborne waited, not sure how to open the conversation. She spoke first, "That man is mean, Grandpa. I don't like him. C.J. is so nice. Why is he so mean?"

"I don't know, hon. But there are a lot of mean people in this world and they can be hard to understand. If it makes you feel better, I don't like him either. For your next lesson on fly fishing, we'll go on my bassboat and invite C.J. Only C.J. How's that sound?"

Mason nodded her head in quiet agreement. Osborne decided to plunge ahead. "Speaking of mean—I'll never forget how, when I was a little older than you are today and away at boarding school, there was a boy in the fourth grade who was a big bully. Always beating up on the younger, smaller kids. The boys in his dorm were scared to death but no one would tell the grown-ups what he was doing. He said he would kill them if they told on him."

Osborne shook his head, "Those younger boys were terrified."

"Did he hurt you?" Mason's eyes were wide.

"No, because I was living in a different dorm. And I was older than the bully so he might not have picked on me anyway. But one of my friends was in the bully's dorm and when he heard what was happening, he got upset. He got really upset when he found out that other boys—older boys like him—knew what was happening but they didn't do anything to stop the bullying either."

Osborne patted Mason's knee. "They were older but they were scared, too."

"But your friend wasn't?"

"Oh, I imagine he had to be kind of scared, but he was willing to take a chance if it meant protecting the younger boys."

"Did he tattle?"

"Yes, he did. He decided it was better to be called a tattletale—if that might happen—than to see kids hurt. Depends on how you look at it, Mason. I call stopping bad people 'whistle blowing'—and that is very different from tattling about something small, because when you 'blow the whistle' you are *helping* to stop something that is very wrong and hurting people."

Silence from the girl on the log beside him. Osborne decided to press on: "Would you like to know how he made up his mind to blow the whistle on that bully?"

Mason nodded.

"He did it because his grandmother had told him once that she didn't care if he grew up to be rich and famous so much as she hoped he would be kind and brave—brave enough to help people who might not be able to help themselves. And that's what he thought about when he heard the younger boys were getting picked on and no one was doing anything about it: *was this a time to be brave?*"

"Ray is brave." Mason sat up a little taller. "He stopped Mr. Calverson."

"He sure did. You know … Chief Ferris and I think you're brave, sweetheart."

Mason studied his face, eyes questioning, then she glanced away as she dug at the dirt and pebbles with her sandals.

"Brave enough to tell me what happened this morning so other kids don't get hurt."

Mason shrugged and tried to change the subject: "You mean Lewellyn?"

"Yes, my good friend Lewellyn—she likes you."

"You mean your *girlfriend* Lewellyn?"

"I don't know about that," said Osborne, grinning. "You'll have to ask her."

Mason continued to stare at her feet, determined not to meet his gaze. Darn, thought Osborne, he had said the wrong thing.

"That kid at your school—the one that, um, blew the whistle. What happened to him?"

"He's a pediatrician, well, just retired. A doctor for little kids. Oh, wait, you mean did something bad happen to him after he told the priests what was going on?"

Mason nodded.

"No. When the grown-ups heard what was happening, they called the bully into the principal's office right away and the principal called his parents. He was not allowed to spend one more night in the dorm, but was sent home that day.

"Boy, was our school relieved to be able to put a stop to the bullying. And my friend did not get hurt, no one called him a tattletale. The younger boys are all grown up today, of course, but when we have school reunions—they still thank him.

"It isn't easy to be brave, Mason, but it's one of the most important things you can ever do. By the way, since you mentioned Chief Ferris, I'll tell you a secret—I can only call her 'Lewellyn' when she's not working. This is professional law enforcement so I have to use her official title. Is that okay with you?"

"Promise not to tell Mom?"

"Why, sweetheart? She's worried to death about you."

"Grandpa, last week she hollered at Dad that she has enough to worry about. She said one more thing and she'll have a nervous breakdown. I don't want to make her have a nervous breakdown."

Osborne had to put his head down to hide his smile. When had Erin not blown things out of proportion? She would be so mad at herself if she knew the effect that marital spat had had on her daughter.

"Honeybunch, I promise I can help your mom avoid a nervous breakdown. But the fact is that if we don't tell her something, she'll continue to worry and that's not good either. Now how about you tell me what happened, than I'll tell Chief Ferris and together we'll decide what to tell your mom. Does that work?"

Mason was quiet for a long time. Finally she said in a tiny little voice, "Grandpa, I think it's my fault because I have impure thoughts sometimes and Sister Frances said that impure thoughts can make bad things happen to you."

"Oh, so this might have something to do with the private parts of your body." Osborne kept his tone level as his worry skyrocketed.

"Yes. Kind of. Not mine—someone else's."

"Whose?"

"The big boy at the fish pond."

"Did he touch you?"

"No. But he really scared me." Mason jumped to her feet as she said, "Grandpa, he was on the island with no clothes on. He kept showing me ... you know?"

"His bottom?" Osborne chose the word Mary Lee had always used with their daughters.

Mason's head nodded up and down.

"But that's not your fault. What scared you? Did he get close to you?"

"I don't know. I was afraid he would cross the island and come after me so I ran and then I saw someone on a bike and ... and ... I think it could've been him."

"So that's why you hid?"

"Yes."

"But he didn't touch you?"

She shook her head 'no.'

"Are you afraid to go back to the fish pond?"

"Yes." It was a whisper.

"Okay, here's what we do. First, I will let your mom know you're okay. That's as much as I'll say—no one has touched you or hurt you. Then I'll talk to Chief Ferris and she'll have her officers watch the island and the fishpond so no other little kids are frightened. And next time you want to go to the fishpond? I'll go with you. *As often as you need me to.* Does that make you feel better?"

The relief on his granddaughter's face brought Osborne close to tears. "Brave of you to tell me, sweetheart," he said, patting her hand. "Hungry?"

"Hot dogs!" shouted Mason as she ran back along the path. Osborne exhaled, then followed.

Life in his world was certainly never boring: Nervous breakdowns, impure thoughts, and the logic of children. Jeez Louise. He could sure as hell use a hot dog, himself.

CHAPTER 16

Osborne dropped Mason off shortly after six, managing with a few quick whispers to let Erin know only that she had been frightened by a "big boy" exposing himself.

"Oh, Dad …"

"But not touched. From a distance. The kid was standing out on that island across from the fishpond. She's okay."

"Thank goodness," said Erin, relief flooding her face. "Are you telling the cops or do you want me to?"

"Let me talk to Lew first," said Osborne. "There's nothing to be done tonight anyway, and she's out with friends in town for their high school reunion. She knows how worried we've been, and she told me to call tonight if I found out more. So I'll give her a call later."

"Good. If I know Lewellyn Ferris, she'll put an end to that funny business," said Erin, her mouth grim. "When you find out, let me know who the creep is, will you, Dad? Doesn't hurt for other parents to know we've got a potential sex offender in Loon Lake."

"Now, Erin, the important thing is Mason is okay—she inhaled three hot dogs, a bushel of potato chips and two bottles of root beer. And I've promised to go along to the fishpond with her until we find whoever it was that bothered her. I really think she's okay."

"Thanks, Dad, " said Erin. "I just wish I knew why she wouldn't tell *me*."

"She doesn't want you to have a nervous breakdown. Sound familiar?" Osborne decided not to mention Sister Mary Frances and the impure thoughts.

"Oh, jeez, did I really say that?" Erin scrunched her face in mock pain. "Mom used to say that all the time. I can't believe I did that."

She sure wouldn't do it again, thought Osborne as he drove off. Halfway home and anxious as always to hear Lew's voice if only on her voice mail, he decided to pull over and give her a call on his cell phone. No doubt she was at dinner but at least he could leave a message and hope she might call sooner rather than later.

To his surprise, she answered. He could hear the buzz of a restaurant in the background but Lew seemed eager to take the call. He pictured her leaving the table and walking over to a quiet place to talk to him. He liked the feeling.

"That's good news and bad news, Doc," she said after hearing that Mason had been frightened but not physically harmed. "We had a similar situation on the island several years ago and the city put up new fencing specifically to keep people out. Sounds like that fence has been vandalized.

"Roger's on duty tonight. I'll have the switchboard call him right now. Ask him to check on it and arrange for a maintenance crew to get there first thing in the morning. I doubt Mason is the only child who's been frightened. You're sure she's okay?"

"I think so. She enjoyed the picnic. Ray entertained everyone," said Osborne. "Hey, sounds like you're having a good time …" He tried to keep his tone lighthearted.

"I am. So great to see everyone. But next time we all get together, I want you along. My friends would like to meet you."

"Really?" Osborne grinned into the cell phone.

"Oh—and the Wausau boys are sending one of their guys—remember Bruce? He'll be in town first thing in the morning. He's been fishing up in Sylvania and was due back in the offices tomorrow anyway. I expect him in my office around eight a.m. Can you be there, too? Stand in for our missing coroner?"

"Sure."

"Oops, here comes Greg—I better say goodbye."

"Greg—is that the millionaire home builder?" Osborne dared to ask the question.

"That's Greg. He's invited me to join him in the Bahamas—Lovely Bay. Wants to show me how to catch bonefish with a fly rod."

"Must be an expert, huh?" Osborne's heart hit the floor of his Subaru.

"Expert on martinis, for sure—he's on his fourth. And you know I don't handle *that* real well. I told him when he dries out … maybe. He didn't care for the comment." As if she knew what Osborne was thinking, she gave a low chuckle, "I have my hands full with you, Doc—in the water and out of the water. See you first thing in the morning?"

"I'll be there."

"Bye." The softness in her voice … he was glad he had called. The martinis considered, he was no longer worried.

———

Seated near the bar of the Bobcat Inn, Osborne studied the menu although he had known walking in what he would order. "Paul," said Mary Lee, her voice petulant, "tell Abe he has to move us—we are regular customers and I do *not* want to sit at the bar. I mean, it's impossible to see anyone." You mean you can't be seen, thought Osborne, but kept his mouth shut.

"Honey, we got here late and I don't see an empty table," he said. Mary Lee huffed and slammed her menu down. They usually sat at one of four tables set against the far wall and in front of an expanse of picture windows overlooking the lake—and the dining room. Osborne was well aware that his wife liked to spend more time checking out who was dining with whom than observing loons.

As determined as Mike chewing on one of Osborne's favorite chamois gloves, Mary Lee was not about to give up. She leapt from her chair, tossed her purse to Osborne and pointed. A member of her bridge club had just been seated with her husband—at one of the *right* tables. "I'll just see if Janie and Herb will let us join them."

As Mary Lee crossed the room, a tinkling from the bar prompted Osborne to shift his chair for a better angle. He liked this table. It offered a front row view of the Bobcat Inn's Friday night "special" that had been charming Loon Lake residents and tourists for years: Abe Conjurski playing musical medleys on an assortment of bar glasses with a cocktail stirrer.

While Abe entertained patrons of the restaurant with his tinkling renditions of classic tunes, his wife Patsy along with one other waitress—the two of them wiping the sweat from their foreheads—would bustle in and out of the kitchen with plate after plate of beer-battered walleye or perch, Patsy's special cole slaw, and "your choice" of French fries or potato pancakes. For the Bobcat, Friday night fish fry was the most profitable night of the week.

The Osbornes ate there at least twice a month even though Mary Lee whined every time: "Pa-a-u-l, you know all our friends are at the Loon Lake Pub—and the Pub has a better fish fry, too. At least you get a choice of salads."

"But they don't have Abe and his music," Osborne would remind her, "and keep in mind, Mary Lee, that Abner and Patsy Conjurski are patients of mine. It's important that we patronize the Bobcat." That was one of the few arguments he won.

———

Osborne's eyes flew open. He blinked. A muffled roar of thunder. He lay still, getting his bearings. The dream had seemed so real, he had to make sure it was a dream. But, of course, it was. It's been over two years since Mary Lee passed away.

Abe and Patsy have been gone longer than that—and the Bobcat Inn closed for years. He was wide awake now, remembering how it was that right after Patsy died of a heart attack while waiting tables, poor Abe (Abner might be the name on his dental charts but he went by 'Abe') had disappeared.

That's right, thought Osborne. Abe had gone off the deep end, not unlike Osborne himself in the months following Mary Lee's death. Drinking out of those glasses instead of playing them. Then Abe had started to hit the casinos. Without Patsy to help him run the restaurant and keep life in order, he was a lost soul. One weekend he was gone for good and it was rumored that he had flown to Vegas with a hooker from Chicago.

A couple distant relatives made feeble attempts around town to ask questions but finally they gave up. With Patsy gone and no close heirs, the restaurant was dismantled and the furnishings sold off, which is how his rug must have ended up at Nystrom's antique store.

Osborne wasn't sure if Abe Conjurski had ever been officially declared dead. Luckily for Osborne, he had managed to avoid Abe's fate. His destination, determined by his daughters, was not casinos but what the three of them now referred to as 'Intervention City' followed by a stint at Hazelden and, ever since, a weekly meeting in the room behind the door with the coffee pot etched in the glass: a rerouting for which he gave thanks every morning.

Osborne turned over to go back to sleep, then turned back, threw off the blanket and jumped to his feet. That's right! Abe had been a patient. Why hadn't he thought of that earlier? What a numbskull. If he hadn't been so preoccupied with worry over Mason, it would have dawned on him right away.

Not only that, but the dental records for Abe Conjurski had to be in one of the file cabinets in back of his garage. That skull, those fillings, no wonder he'd had a sense of déjà vu. Not that the remains might have anything to do with Abe, but it was certainly worth ruling out the possibility.

Osborne's file cabinets had been a sore issue with Mary Lee. When he sold his practice to a young dentist who planned to keep electronic records, she had insisted that he get rid of all his paper files, the x-rays and his office furniture. Osborne knew better than to argue but he wasn't ready to let go.

Where his wife saw a manila file that deserved to be tossed in the garbage, he saw a person, someone he had treated through good times and difficult times in their life. He saw their family, he saw their signature on a check, he saw the venison chops they used for barter when funds were low. His dental files were not just files, they were tokens of the profession that he had loved.

However he may have disappointed Mary Lee as a husband, he had rarely disappointed a patient. He had been a very good dentist.

So he had conspired with Ray to have the tall oak file cabinets, each drawer holding the original files and dividers, delivered on a day when Mary Lee was on a day trip with her bridge club. Working fast, they had put up sheet rock at the very back of the garage—right behind the area where he stored the snow blower, lawn equipment, outboard motor, canoe and gas grill during the winter months.

A few days later, they were able to cut a doorway into the attached shed that he used for cleaning fish. Since Mary Lee alleged she could smell fish guts just walking by the shed windows, there was minimal risk she would violate his space: the files were safe. And—since he had met Lew and been deputized to take over whenever Pecore was recovering from having been over-served or had sunk to new levels of incompetence—they had proved more valuable than he had ever expected.

---

Once he was on his feet, Osborne moved so fast he tripped over the dog. Mike reared up, eyes curious and tail thumping on the floor. He needed out.

Fine, an excellent excuse to check for Abe's file right now. He pulled on his robe and headed for the back door. It was three in the morning with a soft rain falling. So what if he got his feet wet? Lew was expecting him for the morning meeting with Bruce from the Wausau Crime Lab and who knows what he might find. Or not.

CHAPTER 17

Bruce Peters and Osborne pored over the yellowing dental chart, shoulders touching as they stood side by side in the morgue at St. Mary's Hospital. This wasn't the first time they had worked together in the hospital's morgue, the use of which would be billed to the Loon Lake Police Department on an hourly basis.

"Looks pretty damn good to me," said the young forensic specialist. He turned raised eyebrows to Osborne.

Osborne swore Bruce spent his life with his eyebrows raised: in query, in joking, in sheer wonderment over women and fish. A year ago, he'd discovered fly fishing and the love of his life simultaneously (the girl of his dreams had spotted him in the Prairie River taking a casting lesson from Lew and decided right then that she would marry him)—upon which he took to badgering Lew on both subjects.

She answered the fishing questions, but when he puzzled over his newfound love life she would give a sly grin and pass him off to Osborne—who was no help whatsoever and suspected he was being set up.

At first Osborne had resented the younger man, seeing him as an interloper siphoning off too much of Lew's time and possibly flirting. After all, if Osborne was dazzled by her skills in the trout stream—and constantly amazed at the effect her dark eyes had on him—wouldn't every man feel that way? Would age make a difference?

But after working together on a tough murder case the previous winter, he came to see Bruce as a big, friendly mutt of a guy: nerdy, skilled and quite competent. A distinct improvement over the general arrogance of the other Wausau boys who were addicted to making dumb jokes about women in law enforcement.

More important, he was eager to barter forensic expertise for tips on the art of fly fishing. Now *that* Lew did appreciate, even if it meant dealing with a tsunami of questions having little to do with the investigation at hand.

"Sure, Chief Ferris, I can handle the forensics on that break-in," Bruce would say, only to follow with, "if you promise to tell me what might be hatching on the Elvoy tomorrow night … Oh, and which of these trout flies did you say would work best? Hey, take a look at my fly line—do I need a new leader? Think my 5-weight fly rod is too light for muskies?" And so it would go, but a dozen queries later Lew would have the forensics done and a pristine chain of custody protecting any evidence.

Bruce might be a nuisance, but as his fishing skills improved so did Lew's budget for assistance from the Wausau Crime Lab.

———

Osborne laid the cardboard strip holding a set of full-mouth x-rays labeled "Abner Conjurski" alongside the notes he had written in longhand twelve years ago. Then he and Bruce strolled over to the autopsy table on which rested the skull that had fallen out of the rug at the antique shop. The jaw was intact with its three gold inlays gleaming under the overhead lights. The inlays were undeniably the artistry of Dr. Paul Osborne: he knew it and the chart proved it.

"Abe was one of my few patients willing to pay for gold," said Osborne, "he was a practical man and believed me when I said the inlays would hold up better than any amalgams—and I was right!"

"Sure makes this easier," said Bruce, leaning over the skull with calipers out to doublecheck his measurements. A rustling from behind prompted Osborne to look back over his shoulder. Lew had entered the room and stood just inside the door, her arms folded. She motioned for them to continue.

"I think we got it," said Osborne as much to her as to Bruce.

"This is your man, all right," said Bruce. "No question about it. Hey, Chief, Doc and I got this done so fast do you think you can cover for me if I scoot north and get in a half day on the Middle Ontonagon River?"

"You tell me what Wausau needs to hear and I'll make it happen," said Lew, adding in a semi-stern voice, "so long as it doesn't cost me."

"Hell, no, I can fix that. I'll just finish the paperwork so we can have the remains and the rug sent down to the lab for analysis to determine cause of death and any other anomalies. You know the lab work may take a few weeks, right?"

"Of course," said Lew, "but we've got an ID, which helps us enormously. If you're confident we've got all the evidence we need from the antique store?"

"Let the poor guy reopen. That rug has been there so many years that you've got one hell of a compromised crime scene— not to mention that it's highly unlikely the victim died there.

"Oh, I have a question," said Bruce, squinting as if he was in pain. "This college buddy of mine swears that nymphing is the *only* way to fly fish these days. He said everyone he fishes with thinks nymphing is the way to go. But, jeez, I've tried it and I hate it. I like dry flies. Is there something wrong with me?"

"Bruce," said Lew, "not wanting to nymph is hardly a character flaw. I don't nymph," she said throwing both hands in the air. "Doc here doesn't nymph."

"I don't know what that is," said Osborne, interrupting. Lew gave him a look indicating he should shut up.

"Your friend is nuts," said Lew. "There are no hard and firm rules—you choose your trout fly by the hatch and what kind of water you're fishing. Now, Bruce, you're a big boy— fish how you want to fish. Don't listen to bullshit from some pretentious jabone. You know better than that."

As Bruce's squint of pain morphed into confidence, Lew chuckled. "Look, you did me a big favor getting down here first thing this morning, so let me give you a Grizzly King that was tied by an old friend of my uncle's. It's all my uncle would ever fish with and it can be fished wet or dry. I'll put two in the box so you'll still have one after you snag that branch you love. And I'll add a dry fly I've had good luck with this summer—a Size 12 Renegade."

"Really?" Bruce was so delighted his eyebrows hit the ceiling.

"Yeah, well, now you owe me, kiddo."

Lew turned to Osborne, "Doc, I drove over because I just had a call from your daughter, Erin. She has an emergency of some kind. Wouldn't say what on the phone—said it would take some explaining. I told her to come right in. Since it could be about your granddaughter, I thought you might want to be there."

Erin was waiting when they walked into the building. She was dressed in a black pantsuit and holding a briefcase in one hand. Osborne recognized the look in her eyes: grim determination. Could she have found the boy who frightened Mason?

"Erin, you look ready to send someone to the state pen," said Osborne, half joking.

"This isn't about Mason, Dad—but some disturbing news about C.J.'s husband."

"Oh," said Osborne, "if you're referring to the incident on the boat yesterday, I'm sorry I didn't bring it up but we had enough going on. Wouldn't you say it's really a personal issue for the couple?"

As they walked down the hallway to Lew's office, Erin said, "When Mason told me about Calverson being so nasty to his wife, I thought it might be wise for me to take action on something involving Curt Calverson that I've been working on for the last two weeks. It's not about his relationship with his wife, Dad. It's even more serious."

"Come in, come in," said Lew as they entered her office. "Let's sit over there." She pointed to the seating area under the windows facing the courthouse lawn where a sofa, two chairs, and a coffee table made it easy to talk. A light breeze carried the scent of mock orange in bloom. Erin opened her briefcase and pulled out a small stack of papers and what appeared to be direct mail brochures.

"Chief Ferris, you know I've decided to do Legal Aid work until Cody is in first grade because they let me set my own hours?"

Lew nodded, so Erin went on. "Well, I was approached several weeks ago by an elderly woman from Tomahawk, Dolores Rotier. She was convinced someone had stolen money from her bank account because she couldn't use her ATM card to make a withdrawal. That wasn't the problem, really. Dolores didn't understand there was a limit to what she could withdraw in a day but even so, the amount she was allowed to withdraw was so small that I thought the situation was worth looking into.

"I learned that for the last eighteen months, she has been paying on loans from Calverson Finance."

"As in *Curt* Calverson?" asked Osborne.

"Right, Dad, it's a finance company run by C.J.'s husband. Dolores told me she is one of several elderly residents she knows who got a brochure like this in the mail last year." C.J.

waved one of the brochures. "She called the number in the
ad and was told that Calverson Finance would give her a
good deal on a loan if she agreed to have her $550 monthly
government aid check deposited directly into a new account
with them.

"So she did. She agreed to the direct deposit and then ap-
plied for a loan of $204.84 for a couch. The whole set-up
sounded fishy to me and Dolores is certainly no financial wiz-
ard, which is why I decided to investigate further. That's when
I discovered that the finance company also charged her
$75.00 for death and dismemberment insurance and an addi-
tional $10.00 insurance fee. Add interest charges to that and
it seems she now owed Calverson Finance $360.00, which she
had agreed to pay in monthly installments of $72.00.

"That's not all. Six months ago, she gets another loan of
$167.00 because she had surgery and extra bills. This time
Calverson Finance adds a car-club membership for $90.00.
But Dolores doesn't own a car, she can't drive and she never
knew she was buying the membership. Also, she is never told
that there is an additional monthly fee of $4.99 just for the di-
rect deposit.

"When she came to me, she thought she had two small
loan payments. That's why she couldn't understand why she
couldn't withdraw some of her government aid money—
enough for groceries—with the ATM card the bank sent her.

"Chief Ferris, Dad, this is not about two small loan
payments—Dolores Rotier is in her late eighties and she now
owes nearly all the money she receives monthly to Calverson

Finance. When I add up their fees and interest, this poor elderly lady is paying an effective annual percentage rate of around 94 percent! Is this a scam or what?"

It was a rhetorical question; Erin wasn't finished. "We checked with Legal Aid in a couple more towns around here—Rhinelander, Eagle River, Woodruff—and found nine more elderly people in the same fix. Turns out Calverson sent fliers to all the old folks getting government benefits, encouraging the direct deposit of their monthly checks and touting the wonderful loans they could get."

"Erin," said Lew, "there is nothing the Loon Lake Police can do about this. Bank fraud is a federal crime—not under our jurisdiction. You need the F.B.I. But I must warn you that if the small print on the documents you have there—"

"I know, I know. I'm working with some of my colleagues at Legal Aid who know more about financial issues to draw up a formal complaint, but that takes time. Meanwhile people like Dolores are at the mercy of this man."

"Can she close her account?"

"Not until she pays what she owes—but I am working on canceling her direct deposit. Chief Ferris, the guy's a creep. Even if you can't do anything, I feel you should know what he's up to. I mean, hey, you keep track of the drug dealers, may as well keep track of this guy, don't you think?"

"You're right. We do need to know this is happening. But, again, it's the FBI who really needs to know."

"Any Loon Lake residents doing business with this firm?" asked Osborne.

"That's why I'm here, Dad. Old Mr. Gilley and Mrs. Schradtke. Mr. Gilley's too embarrassed to file a complaint and Mrs. Schradtke's short term memory problems are making it very difficult to help her. Her neighbor is the one who called us."

"Wait. *Are we talking about Bobby Schradtke's mother?*" Lew asked.

"Yes," said Erin, getting to her feet and slipping the papers back into her briefcase.

"Keep me informed on this, will you please?" asked Lew.

"Sure. Thanks for listening," said Erin.

After she left the office, Osborne turned to Lew. "Well, that was interesting."

"Interesting and frustrating. I sure wish there was more that this department could do for those older folks ..." Lew shrugged, "but, like I said, the Feds are in charge when it comes to bank fraud.

"Meanwhile, I *can* do something about Abe Conjurski now that you and Bruce have ID'd his remains. Let's go downstairs and look for the files from the year he disappeared. Twelve years ago? Let's hope they aren't in one of those boxes that Pecore had to take down to Madison."

CHAPTER 18

On entering the basement storeroom with its narrow aisles of wooden shelving reaching up to the ceiling, Osborne and Lew each chose an aisle, scanning along the shelves for the cardboard file box that should hold case files for the year that Abe Conjurski had disappeared.

"I wasn't on the force then," said Lew, "but I'm sure we'll find at least a missing person report. Too bad these haven't been scanned into the system, but maybe one of these days …" She walked slowly, checking the dates scribbled in black marker onto the fronts of the long boxes.

"Hey, this might be it," she said, pulling at one. "Doc, would you give me a hand please? This box must weigh over fifty pounds. Should be a list in the front that indicates all the cases stored inside."

"By date or alphabetical?"

"Both, I believe. I haven't had a reason to look in these since the city council decided to save money and space by having the department transfer inactive case files from the old metal file cabinets to these. I'll tell you, Doc, all this does is remind me we need a new building, new computers, and more staff—but that's not likely to happen."

Tugging together, they hoisted the long, heavy box from the shelf and were easing it onto the floor when Lew's cell phone rang.

"Yes, Marlene, what is it?" she said on seeing that the call was from the switchboard upstairs. "Right. Where? Let the EMTs know I'm on my way." She clipped the phone back on her belt and turned to Osborne. "911 dispatcher just called. We've got a rollover north of town. Victim called from the vehicle. Dispatcher thinks someone may be pinned inside.

"With Todd off today and Roger working a break-in at the Dog House Tavern—afraid it's up to me, Doc. We'll have to do this later." She was out the door and running up the stairs as she spoke.

"Need help?" Osborne asked, hurrying behind her.

"Wouldn't hurt, especially if we beat the EMTs to the site."

---

As the cruiser sped in the direction given by the 911 dispatcher, Osborne spotted familiar road signs: they were headed towards Big Moccasin Lake. Sure enough, they turned off the county highway onto a gravel road and, two fire numbers later, started down the long driveway that led to a house he had visited less than twenty-four hours earlier.

"Y'know," he said, "I'm pretty sure we're on our way to the Calverson's." No sooner had he spoken than they rounded a sharp curve and Osborne shouted, "Watch out!"

Lew hit the brakes and yanked the steering wheel hard to the right to avoid rear-ending a Toyota Land Cruiser parked upside down at an angle across the narrow, heavily wooded lane. The way the car had flipped but missed the wall of Norway pines lining the drive was amazing to Osborne. "Wow, are they lucky," he said.

"You mean—are *we* lucky," muttered Lew.

The front door on the passenger side hung wide open but all they could see was the backside of a woman on her knees, her torso deep inside the car. "She could be pinned," said Lew. "Let's hope she's not hurt bad."

"That has to be C.J. in the car. I see Curt Calverson over there," said Osborne, pointing to a man on the far side of the overturned vehicle who was marching back and forth, his eyes on them as he waved one arm while shouting into his cell phone.

"Your wife—is she hurt?" cried Lew, leaping from the police cruiser.

"My goddamn car is totaled," said Curt, slamming his phone shut and spitting out the words. Osborne couldn't tell if the man's face was red with anger or if he had survived a face plant on the windshield.

"That's not what I asked," said Lew. "Is your wife—"

"I'm shook up, but nothing serious," said the woman from inside the car as she backed her way out and got to her feet. It was C.J. "I was just looking for my purse. I know I'm okay and Curt seems … well, upset but—"

"Okay, hold on both of you," said Lew. "The EMTs are on their way. They'll make sure you don't need medical assistance. She reached for her cell phone to place a quick call to Marlene to request a tow truck. She looked over at the Calversons, who were still standing on opposite sides of their overturned car. "Who was driving?"

"Me, but that's not the point here," said Curt. "Someone tried to kill me. This was attempted murder, and I sure as hell expect you people to get off your butts and do something—"

"Whoa, bud, calm down," said Lew. "Looks to me like you rolled your car taking that curve too fast. Your wheels hit gravel and …"

As Lew spoke, C.J. raised both arms, waving her hands to beckon them towards the front of the large SUV. "Chief Ferris," said Osborne, pointing at C.J. as he jogged around the front of the vehicle, "this is Mrs. Calverson—C.J. She's the woman who helped Mason yesterday."

He rounded the front of the vehicle only to stop so fast that he and Lew nearly collided. They stared down in stunned silence. A deer, a large dead deer—a buck with its antlers covered in velvet—lay on the road in front of the SUV. The rear flanks of the dead animal were pinned under the vehicle and not visible. "Whoa, that's one heck of a road kill," said Osborne.

"I hit the brakes hard as I could but my front bumper caught it—that's when we flipped," said Curt. "That damn thing was right smack in the middle of the road as we came around the curve. I'm damn lucky to be alive. If we hadn't rolled, we'd have hit those trees at forty miles an hour!"

"You are very lucky, indeed," said Lew, her voice quiet and eyes thoughtful as she took in the car, the distance it had rolled and the position of the dead deer.

"Tell me something, Curt," said Osborne, his own close calls in mind, "was the deer traveling as you came around the curve? Do you recall if *you* hit the deer—or did the deer hit you?"

"Didn't you hear what I said? The goddamn deer wasn't moving," said Curt, arms up and hands flailing as he stomped back and forth along one side of the SUV.

Hmm, thought Osborne. He caught Lew's eye and knew they were both thinking the same thing: if this imitation of Rumpelstiltskin continued much longer, the EMTs might have their hands full after all.

"What I am trying to tell you is that dead deer was already there—lying right in the middle of the goddamn road when we came around the bend. *Some asshole put it there.*"

"Mr. Calverson. Please stop your shouting," said Lew, her tone gracious. "I am standing right here and I can hear you just fine."

"Listen," Curt choked twice before he could speak, "my wife and I drove out of here less than two hours ago and there was no dead animal in the road at that time. You think I'm making this up? Where is the State Patrol? I want a serious investigation—not some local yahoos."

"Thank you," said Lew, continuing to keep her voice remarkably even—at least in Osborne's opinion. By now he would've punched the guy. And if the idiot kept it up that might still be an option.

"Mr. Calverson, let's start over and try to remain calm. I may be a 'local yahoo' but it so happens I am also the Chief of the Loon Lake Police Department. Lewellyn Ferris is my name, and this accident is under my jurisdiction. For the record, I make the decision to call in the county sheriff if needed—not the State Patrol. Dr. Osborne here is one of my deputies—"

"I've met Osborne," said Curt with a grunt. "So what the hell are you going to do? How the hell do I get my car out of here and what are you going to do about ... about ... that!" He whirled around to jab an angry finger towards the animal carcass.

"Curt, honey, please settle down or you'll have another heart attack," said C.J.

Her husband wheeled on her: "How many times do I have to tell you to shut your fucking mouth!"

"Mr. Calverson," said Lew, stepping towards him, "I want you in the patrol car. Now." She pointed at the car. "Leave the doors open so you get plenty of air and I suggest you sit quietly and take few deep breaths. Your wife can join you if she wishes. Meanwhile, Dr. Osborne and I will take a good look at the damage here and then I'll need to ask you some questions for the report."

"What do you mean a *report*? No one is hurt. I don't need a report—my insurance will cover this."

"Any time there is over a thousand dollars worth of damage to a vehicle, I have to file a report. Now, to answer your questions—a tow truck is on its way and I will arrange for someone to remove the carcass."

C.J. stepped forward from where she had been standing near the front of the car. "Curt ..." her voice trembled, "would it help if I called our insurance company while you talk to Chief Ferris?"

"Oh, for Chrissake," said Curt, waving his hands in defeat. He marched over to the police cruiser, slid into the back seat, laid his head back and closed his eyes. C.J. found a stump in the shade behind the cruiser and sat down. Elbows on her knees, she buried her face in her hands. Osborne thought he saw her shoulders shaking.

Lew waited until both were settled before motioning for Osborne to follow as she knelt down beside the deer. They didn't have to get very close to see Curt was right about one thing: the animal had been dead long enough that maggots were feasting. Lew got to her feet and took a slow stroll along the road, studying the patterns in the gravel.

"Look here, Doc," she said, her eyes focused on a patch of gravel and weeds, "you can see where that deer was dragged in from behind those pines. Any chance you know where Ray is this morning? I'd sure like to see if he can help us out—follow those tracks on back into the woods. I'd like to know how that animal got here."

"I'll try his cell, if he's not out of range, he'll answer."

"Yo, Doc? What's up?" asked a happy baritone within seconds. Osborne handed his phone to Lew.

"Ray, I need your services ASAP," she said. "Where are you right now?"

"Oh, just standin' in my kitchen fryin' up a batch of fresh-caught bluegills for my buddy, Nick, here. Got enough for four—you and the old man want to join us?"

"Thanks but no thanks," said Lew. She spoke fast, describing the scene and what was needed. "Since we had that rain last night, I think there's a decent chance of finding some sign of how and when this animal was dumped here. Pay you for your time, of course."

"You said the magic words," said Ray, "Mind if I make it an ed ... u ... cational op-p-p ... or ... tunity for my friend here? Nick invited me to pre-fish Big Moccasin with him and his buddies later this afternoon so we were heading that way anyhoo. Do you mind if I bring him along?"

"Not if you'll eat fast and meet us here," said Lew. "Shouldn't take me more than fifteen minutes to get what I need from the Calversons for the police report. Doc and I will stay until you arrive. I don't want the tow truck moving anything before you get here."

Lew snapped the phone shut, saying, "That was easy. Ray should be on his way in a few minutes." Then she headed over to the police cruiser to speak to the Calversons while Osborne decided to take one more look at the upside down Land Cruiser.

He ruminated as he studied the car: Interesting that Ray would drop whatever he was doing to get here so soon. The only time he could get the guy to move fast was when he had a fish on the line. Could it be the presence of the lovely C.J.? Might be a good idea to mention that to Lew ... just in case it could complicate matters, which it shouldn't. But then Ray is Ray.

Osborne knelt to examine the deer again. No marks on the carcass that he could see. It didn't appear the animal had been hit by another vehicle, which was curious since hunting season was months away. Just as he was pondering the size of the animal and if it had taken more than one person to drag the carcass, C.J. walked up. "Doc," she said, keeping her voice very low, "does Erin handle divorce cases?"

"Not that I know of," said Osborne, looking up in surprise. Seeing the expression in C.J.'s eyes, he quickly added, "But if she doesn't, I'm sure she'll know someone who does."

"He just ... he treats me with such contempt," said C.J., pressing her fingers against her eyes as if to hold back tears. "I never expected it to be this way."

Osborne got to his feet. He glanced over the young woman's head to be sure her husband was still talking with Lew. He still was—sitting sideways with his back to them. Osborne reached an arm across C.J.'s shoulders to give her a quick hug. In her jeans and t-shirt, blond hair pulled back in a ponytail, she reminded him of a younger Erin: poor kid, if only he could wipe away those tears and make everything okay.

CHAPTER **19**

Osborne didn't recognize the yellow Honda Civic pulling in behind the tow truck until Ray and Nick got out. "Good, you're just in time," said Lew. She was standing near the carcass that was still wedged under the car. "Ray, would you please take a look at this dead animal before the car is lifted?"

"Okedoke," said Ray, motioning to Nick to wait by the Honda. He walked over to join Lew in front of the overturned SUV. Feet apart, hands thrust into the pockets of his khaki shorts, he studied the dead animal, then turned to walk the same path Lew had walked half an hour earlier.

"Oh, yeah," said Ray, pointing, "look at that. Sure enough, that animal was dragged along here." He knelt to touch the ground. "Tell you right now I'll have no problem finding good tracks in this dirt. Plenty moist still. Okay, Chief," he said, getting to his feet, "I've seen enough. You can let Tony go ahead and move the car."

Lew signaled the tow truck driver and the Land Cruiser made its way up and over and onto the bed of the tow truck. Curt, watching from the sidelines, grimaced at the sight of the damage to the roof. C.J. stood in silence, her arms crossed as she watched not the car, but Ray.

"Hey, now, check *that* out," said Ray, looking down at the lower half of the animal's body, which was now fully exposed. "On the right flank—see what I see?" Osborne and Lew leaned forward together. A small entry wound, a gunshot, was clearly visible. "Is that what you expected?"

"I'm not surprised," said Osborne.

"Me neither. Ray, you know the drill," said Lew, "see if you can track back along the path that animal was dragged. Someone must have thought they were being funny. Likely some teenagers who need to learn just how dangerous a stunt like this can be. Call me as soon as you've got something." With a quick glance, she checked to make sure Curt was listening.

"You got it, Chief. Doc, when I'm done here you want to join me and Nick for the pre-fish?" Ray checked his watch. "Launch from the public landing in an hour and a half?"

"Will you guys be fishing by the island, like yesterday?" said C.J., chiming in. Osborne did a double take: this was a new C.J.—a lively young woman sounding brighter than she had all morning.

"No," said Ray. "I've advised Nick and the boys to pre-fish Susan's Bay. That's the big bay just past the island on the right. There's a short 'no-wake' zone that takes you in there," said Ray.

"Oh sure, I know right where you mean. Good fishing there, huh?"

Ray did not miss the eagerness in C.J.'s eyes and his voice was gentle when he said, "Just the boys today, C.J. We're only allowed five in the boat and we've got two of Nick's team meeting us, too. Don't you worry—Doc and I will get you and Mason out again real soon."

"C.J.!" Curt jabbed a finger in the direction of their house, which was just a quarter of a mile further down the road. They set off together—Curt striding fast, C.J. doing her best to keep up, shoulders slumped.

An hour and a half later, Osborne stood on the dock at the public landing, watching as the black pickup towing the UW team's boat trailer backed its way down to the water. Ray, having parked his truck up behind Osborne's car, sauntered down the gravel road towards the water, spinning rod in one hand, tackle box in the other.

"Hey, Doc, got some interesting news on the Calverson place," said Ray as he joined Osborne. "Our friend, C.J., needs to be careful these days. Someone has been trespassing around their place."

"You're kidding."

"N-o-o, I'm … not." Ray set his gear down to watch with a look of pain on his face as the driver of the team's truck barely managed to avoid backing the rear wheels of the boat trailer into the dock. "No … I am not … kidding." He looked over at Osborne. No smile. "What I found worries me.

"That deer? That sucker had been dragged about fifty feet from where two jabones parked their vehicle—tread marks make me think it might be a Dodge Ram 1500—only they took a little jaunt before making their delivery.

"I tracked their footprints—"

"Two people?"

"Yep. Size of the prints had to be two men in work boots. Tracked 'em through the woods and down to the Calverson place where they came up the side yard, peered through basement windows, then got up on that deck of theirs. Probably tried the doors—I wouldn't be surprised. Too bad Calverson doesn't have a dog. That might've scared 'em off.

"I could be wrong, but the footprints in the yard and around the house were deep enough to make me think they were sneaking around before sun-up—right after the rain had stopped. Then they hung out in the woods until they saw the Calversons drive off.

All I can think, Doc, is what if C.J. had been left alone in that house? I mean, who are these guys and what are they up to?"

"Up to no good from the sound of it," said Osborne.

"Calverson came out of the house while I was checking the tracks in the yard, so I had a brief talk with ol' slugger. Suggested he be sure to keep his security system on. Tried to blow me off, but he can't fool me—that joker's scared." Ray had dropped his signature hesitations.

"Doc, I don't like the feeling I get around that guy. Something is really wrong with that individual. Don't you wonder how a nice girl like C.J.—"

Before he could finish, Osborne said, "I know exactly what you mean. Erin's working with some elderly clients that Calverson's firm has locked into questionable loans. You know, it's beginning to look like the guy is real razzbonya. I assume Lew knows what you found?"

"Left a message with the switchboard. They said she was on her way to meet with Roger—he needed help with a break-in at the Dog House Tavern. Marlene didn't think it was critical enough time-wise to bug her on the cell phone."

---

"Now here's a *real* nice honey hole for bass," said Ray. "I save it for special clients and it's one I've fished any number of times. Caught a five pounder here—" He paused and the three college boys who had been intent on his every word turned to see what it was that had caught his attention. The hum of a jet ski coming around the point and heading their way grew louder.

"Has to been the tenth jet ski we've seen in the last hour," said Osborne. "Let's hope they keep their distance." He wiped the sweat off his forehead as he spoke. The afternoon was so hot and windless under a cloudless sky that he was already planning a dip in the lake the moment he got home. He'd left Mike in the yard, and he hoped the dog had enough water.

"Man, that dude has one cool machine," said Nick, "check it out. I'd like to try one of those!" Osborne had to admit the jet skier looked pretty impressive on his bright yellow machine, a black life vest with a yellow stripe down the back and a full-face orange helmet covered with streaks of black lightning.

"Goddamn fashion statement if you ask me," huffed Ray. "If that jerk gets any closer …" As he spoke the jet ski slowed, keeping its distance as the rider yanked off his helmet and waved to them.

"Hey, that looks like Mrs. Calverson," said Nick, one hand blocking the sun so he could see better. "Yeah, that's no guy—that's that lady friend of yours, Ray."

"Hey, boys," shouted C.J., "want to stop by when you're done and have some cold ones down on our dock—bring your boat over?"

"We'll be out here another hour at least," said Ray, "how 'bout we give you a call when we know how things are going?"

"No problem," said C.J. with a wave. She pulled her helmet back on, fussed with the chin strap, then gave up saying, "I hate this thing. It's too big for me and I can never fasten this damn strap so it's not choking me. Oh well." Letting the chin strap hang unfastened, C.J. gave one more wave as she turned the jet ski around. Kicking up a plume of spray, the watercraft spun away in the direction of the point, back towards the channel and the "No Wake" zone. Feeling lazy in the afternoon heat, Osborne watched through half-lidded eyes as C.J. slowed her jet ski to "no wake" speed.

From the left, on the far side of the point, a dark blue speedboat appeared. From where he stood on the bassboat, Osborne could swear the boat was aimed straight at C.J. But that can't be, he thought, has to be an optical illusion caused by the reflection of the sun off the still water.

The blue boat sped across the surface of the water, clipping the back of the jet ski, which veered right, heading straight for the island.

Osborne held his breath unable to believe what he was seeing. The jet ski hit the shallows and was airborne. "Oh no! Did you—" He turned to Ray but the man was already on his feet shoving Nick from the captain's chair and hitting the throttle as he shouted, "Sit down and hold on!"

CHAPTER 20

As they approached the island, the speedboat that had clipped the back of the jet ski was nowhere to be seen. Ray jumped from the bassboat while the motor was still running. Osborne checked to be sure the ignition was off before jumping into the shallows after Ray.

"Nick, anchor the boat!" He shouted as he pushed as hard and as fast as he could through the knee-high water. He passed the jet ski. It was tipped sideways and rocking in the wake from the bassboat, its engine making burping noises. The helmet must have flown off as its owner was airborne because it was floating near the empty jet ski. On shore—as if flung by a giant hand against an outcropping of boulders and brush—a small figure in a black and yellow life vest lay slumped to one side.

"Don't move her!" said Osborne just as Ray reached to grasp C.J. by the shoulders.

"We have to do *something*. She's vomiting. Oh god, look at her head—what'll we do?" Osborne could see that C.J. appeared to have landed face first on the rocks. She was out cold in spite of the vomiting.

Osborne knelt beside the unconscious C.J. Time stopped as he focused on just one thing: *keep this girl breathing.* "We've got to keep her airway clear—we can't let her choke on the vomit," he said, thankful now for the time he had taken every year to review and practice CPR—just in case he should ever need it for a patient. CPR he could do in his sleep.

His fingers moving to clear the air passage without moving C.J.'s head, he spoke without looking up: "Ray, call 911."

The dispatcher answered within seconds. "We have a severe head injury," said Ray, talking fast and to the point. He gave the location, paused and said, "Victim is unconscious and vomiting." Again he paused to listen. "No, we can't transport by boat because we don't dare move the victim. Can't you send a Life Flight helicopter for a water landing—near the island across from the public landing? They'll see us easy."

This time the dispatcher put him on hold for a brief period. "Okay," said Ray, looking over at Osborne as he repeated what he had just heard.

"So you're saying no helicopter but an ambulance plane with pontoons is on its way from Marshfield Clinic? That'll work." Osborne took a deep breath and hoped. That was good news—if it got here in time.

Ray stayed on the phone answering questions. "The victim is C.J. Calverson, wife of Curt Calverson. Not sure how to reach the husband—they have a house here on Big Moccasin and one in town—"

"Tell them to check with the police department," said Osborne, "Lew filed an accident report on that rollover this morning. All the information should be there."

Ray shut his phone and knelt beside Osborne. Nick and his friends waited in silence off to one side, eyes glued to the two men doing what they could to save a life.

Though it seemed forever to Osborne, it couldn't have been much more than ten minutes before the plane appeared and set down close to shore. Ray and the boys waded out to help the paramedics with their equipment.

"Looks like a possible skull fracture, vital signs—well, hard to tell," said one of the two paramedics into a walkie-talkie after they had strapped C.J. onto a board and were carrying her back to the plane. "Tell the husband we're taking her to the hospital in Rhinelander," were the last words Osborne heard as they disappeared into the plane.

As Osborne, Ray, and the boys boarded the bassboat to head back to the landing, an aluminum fishing boat with a solitary figure headed directly for them. "Can't talk right now, Larry, got an emergency," said Ray to the elderly man with a full beard.

"I know that." Osborne recognized the former owner of a local resort. "But I thought you'd like to know I was fishing off the point back there when I saw that boat come out of nowhere and clip that jet skier—"

"You did? Did you see who was driving? Where they came from?" said Ray.

"Couldn't tell who it was. Fella was wearing sunglasses and one of those safari-type hats pulled down over his face but he knew what he was doing, all right. Jet skier never saw 'em coming I don't think. Came at it from behind and bam! knocked 'er right off track. At high speed, too. Guess he doesn't like jet skis, huh?"

"You didn't happen to see what direction that boat headed off to?" asked Osborne.

"Better'n' that—I got the registration number. Fella took off past the island and on up the east channel there. I saw him earlier. Saw him get in the boat at the Moonlight Bay Resort 'bout twenty minutes ago. Few minutes later, he was cruising up and down along the shoreline right over there." The fisherman pointed towards the shoreline where the Calverson's dock was located.

"Looked to me like he was just waiting for that yellow jet ski. A couple others went by but he didn't bother them. He knew who he was after. Bet you he's way up the chain now, though. Got a pen? Here's the registration number."

"I do," said Nick, ready to write on the back of the lake map he'd been marking earlier. As the man spoke, he wrote fast then read it back to be sure he had it right.

"Catch you later, Larry," said Ray, "likely Chief Ferris will want to talk to you."

"You know where to find me, Ray," said the old guy. He sat and waited for the bassboat to leave.

"Ray, drop me off at Calverson's," said Osborne, "I'll see if Curt's home, and you can pick me up there, okay? I'm going to the hospital."

"Me, too," said Ray. "Nick and the boys can manage. You know, Doc, chances are Calverson is on his stupid phone right when the hospital's trying to call. Give me your car keys and I'll pick you up in your vehicle. We'll go together. Nick, call me later."

"Sure you don't want us to come with you?" asked Nick.

"Boys, right now there's nothing any of us can do. You have a job to do here. I'll keep you posted." Ray gave him a thumbs-up, his face grim.

Dropping Osborne off at the dock minutes later, they all stared at a long, dark blue speedboat resting in its shore station. Without a word, Osborne ran over to check the 150 horsepower outboard on the back. The propeller was dry. The boat had not been in water recently—it wasn't the boat that had hurt C.J.

He waved to the bassboat as it pulled away, then ran up the winding stairs, around to the front of the house and up onto the deck, where he pounded on the door. After a few seconds, Curt appeared in the doorway. "Dr. Osborne, what is it?"

"Your wife has been in an accident and is being flown to the hospital in Rhinelander."

"What?! She was just here a few minutes ago."

"Come with me and I'll explain what happened." As he spoke, Curt's cell phone rang. It was the 911 dispatcher. She had been trying for twenty minutes to reach him.

———

Thirty minutes later, they pulled up to the emergency room entrance at St. Mary's Hospital. "You go with Curt, I'll park the car," said Ray, who had been driving. Osborne and Curt jumped out and ran into the building.

"Mr. Calverson?" asked a nurse as they entered. "Follow me, sir." They followed her to an operating room where medical staff was preparing to work on the still form that had been moved to an operating table.

"Mr. Calverson," said a masked surgeon, "take your wife's hand and say goodbye."

Osborne turned away. He couldn't watch. Curt Calverson froze. He made no move towards his wife. When seconds had passed and Curt still had not moved, Osborne caught the surgeon's eye. He reached for the limp hand, patted it and said softly, "C.J., it's Doc Osborne, and Ray is on his way. We'll be here. Hang in there, kid."

The two men left the room and stepped outside to wait.

CHAPTER 21

C.J. was wheeled into intensive care still unconscious. "We'll know more in twenty-four hours," said the surgeon to Curt and Osborne after meeting them in the waiting room for the families of patients in critical condition. It was after eight.

Lew had arrived while C.J. was in surgery, took notes even though Osborne and Ray could give only the sparse details of the accident, and left. Shortly after, she had called Ray and asked him to meet her at the public landing on Big Moccasin. That had been two hours ago.

The surgeon continued, "When your wife landed on those rocks, she took the brunt of the impact on her forehead. She has a double skull fracture, and the challenge is to manage the swelling of the brain. Fortunately, we happen to be holding a medical retreat here this weekend so the brain trauma team from UW Madison is working with us, too. They know things we don't. She is in good hands."

"Any idea when she will regain consciousness?" asked Curt. Osborne wanted to ask if she would make it, but he knew better than to intrude.

"Hard to say. Not much will change tonight, so I suggest you go home and get some sleep. Now if you'll excuse me, I have another surgery."

Before leaving the room, the surgeon asked one of the surgical nurses to give Curt directions on how to call in to check on his wife's condition.

"How do I reach you if there is a change?" asked the nurse after giving Curt the extension for the nurses' desk in the intensive care unit.

"Don't worry about that," said Curt. "I'll call in."

That's curious, thought Osborne. If it were his family member, he would want to know the slightest change—good or bad. Again he kept his thoughts to himself.

"Curt," said Osborne, "when you know something, I hope you'll let me know how she's doing." Just as he spoke, Lew walked into the waiting room.

"Doc, Mr. Calverson—I was hoping to catch you. We ran a trace on the boat registration and contacted the resort that owns it. It was stolen from their dock shortly before the time you say the accident occurred. We haven't found the boat yet but I've got Ray and one of my officers in boats searching for it. That's a five-lake chain, so unless the boat was trailered out, we should be able to locate it."

"I certainly hope so, and soon," said Curt. "If this doesn't convince you that someone is after me—"

"I understand your feelings, Mr. Calverson," said Lew. "You may be right, or it may be as simple as someone getting into a boat after having too much to drink. I am sorry to say that happens too often up here in the summer. Way too often."

"Well, you're goddamn wrong," said Curt. He turned around to leave, slamming the waiting room door behind him.

"He's right," said Lew, as she and Osborne walked through the hospital corridors towards the parking lot, "someone *is* after him. But not to kill him. Our clerk filed the accident report on the rollover online late this morning and it caught the eye of someone in Madison who passed it along to an insurance investigator in Illinois. He called the office this afternoon.

"The SUV he drives is owned by Calverson Finance, which is headquartered in Illinois. The gentleman who called has been investigating Calverson's firm on behalf of the Illinois Insurance Commission due to consumer complaints of fraud. I told him about Erin's concerns with the elderly folks and their bank deposits. Apparently, that's just what he's been looking for. He's driving up Monday to meet with one of the regional FBI agents—I gave him Erin's name and phone number. I left a message on their home voice mail but I want to be sure she gets it. Will you make sure she knows about this?"

"Of course."

"One more thing, Doc," said Lew, leaning back against the police cruiser and looking up at Osborne with a smile and a pleading look in her eyes, "do you mind helping me out for a short time this evening? I've located five boxes holding files from the year Abe disappeared and I was hoping we could split up the boxes and see if we can't at least pull the right files. I'm off tomorrow and I hate leaving this undone—but you have had a long day."

"*I've* had a long day? Look who was in her office by six this morning. Of course I'll help you out. I'll miss dinner with Mike, but he'll survive. I'll ask Ray to check on him.

"Lew, I'm worried about C.J. A double skull fracture is very, very serious." He shook his head rather than say the worst.

"You like that girl, don't you?"

"She is a sweet kid," said Osborne. "Just a nice, good-hearted young woman. Speaking of good-hearted women, Lewellyn, are we ever going to have some time alone? How 'bout we call it quits at ten and you spend the night at my place?"

She laughed. "Nice try, Doc. Thanks, but not tonight." She chuckled at the crestfallen look on his face. "Tomorrow night works. How's that? I'm taking the day off, working in my garden, and if you'd like, we could take the canoe and our fly rods out on the lake tomorrow evening—catch some bluegills and enjoy a late dinner?"

"O-o-o-kay," said Osborne, wheedling. "What if we find the files right away? Would that change things?"

She punched him in the arm. "See you at the station, Doc."

CHAPTER 22

"We need a better system," said Lew, complaining as she sorted through one of the boxes that they had hoisted onto a long table at one end of the storeroom. "They've stuck everything in here from traffic citations to runaway dogs, for gods sake. The list on the front is worthless—tells you what months are in here and nothing else. Sorry, Doc, this is going to take longer than I thought."

"My box has a good list," said Osborne, glancing over at her. "Alphabetical. You must have had different people organizing these?"

"The mayor made us hire one of his nieces. I think she got her training from Pecore: how to do nothing while getting paid."

Osborne pushed the box in front of him to one side. "Nothing Conjurski-related in June. I'll check July." He leaned over the next box. "Decent list here," he said and thumbed along for about five minutes. He felt happy working under the fluorescent lights with the sound of Lew's soft breathing nearby. "Got one and it's thick."

He handed the file with a small stack of papers inside it to Lew. "Oh, no this isn't about Abe disappearing," she said. "This is a break-in at his restaurant."

———•———

According to the reports in the file, the break-in at the Bobcat Inn was one of seven that occurred around Loon Lake during June and July of that month—and always with the thief or thieves cutting rooftop holes to gain entry. Small businesses were targeted: Moen's Beauty Shop, Birch Bark and More, Taege's Drug Store, McIssac's Books, Leo's Sporting Goods, Little Rock Tavern and the Bobcat Inn.

Items taken were cash, cigarettes, three tackle boxes, fishing lures, cases of beer, a medical bag with a stethoscope and—from the drug store—condoms. The burglary tools were basic: a handsaw and an ax. The burglar or burglars were never apprehended, but the Bobcat Inn was the last of the break-ins that summer.

———•———

Lew looked up from the file, "Doc, you know what's curious here? That break-in that Roger handled earlier today at the Dog House Tavern? Whoever it was used a handsaw and ax to enter. They took cash, cigarettes, an iPod and a laptop computer."

Doc moved his chair close to Lew so he could read over her shoulder as she shuffled through the pages of the police report from the Bobcat. "Look, Abe is still around at this point," said Osborne. "They have his account of finding the cash register smashed. Oh … look at that—whoever it was broke all the glasses he played his tunes on. What a son-ofabitch. To me, that makes it sound like it was somebody who knew Abe. Sheer meanness."

"Get this, Doc," said Lew, pointing to the typed report describing the location and other employees interviewed after the break-in. "Bobby Schradtke was working for Abe at the time of the break-in. I sat in on his probation hearing the other day. That guy is a habitual offender. He's done time for stealing cars, burglaries, possession of burglary tools, aggravated assaults—and that's before this last sentence for distributing crack cocaine.

"Going back to his teen years, he was one mean son of a gun. Before he quit school, he beat up a shop teacher—broke his nose and three ribs."

"I remember reading all the news stories during Schradtke's trial," said Osborne, "but I never knew he worked at the Bobcat Inn. Does that report say what he did there?"

"Dishwasher. He had been arrested for several burglaries and after serving six months, qualified for work release—that's how Abe had hired him. Interesting, huh. Oh … get this—after the break-in at the Bobcat, they searched the trailer where Bobby was living and found axes, a handsaw and a chainsaw, which he claimed he used for logging. Didn't look good, but hardly proof that he was the burglar.

"Okay, let's keep searching for that missing persons report on Abe. Has to be in one of these next two boxes."

Twenty minutes later, they gave up. "I don't understand," said Lew, throwing her hands in the air. "There should be something here."

Osborne checked his watch. It was nine fifteen. "Let me make a quick call to Jack Jarvis, Lew. I noticed on my dental charts that he was Abe's physician and he's a good friend of mine. I don't think it's too late to give him call. Let me see if he remembers the situation then. Is it okay to mention that we've identified Abe's remains?"

Lew nodded an approval.

———⋗•⋖———

"Jack?" said Osborne a moment later. "Sorry to call so late. Chief Ferris and I have a question for you. The Wausau Crime Lab helped us identify some skeletal remains that were found recently—Abe Conjurski. As I recall, you were his physican, weren't you?"

"I was. This is interesting, Doc, I've always wondered what happened to old Abe. He dropped off the face of the earth one day and that was that. Where'd you find the bones—in the woods somewhere?"

"Not exactly," said Osborne. "At this point, let me just say we think it might be foul play. Tell you more when it's official."

"Really sorry to hear that. But, you know, Abe was not a well man after his wife died. He put himself in harm's way. You recall that, don't you?"

"I remember well. What we're trying to figure out is exactly when he disappeared and why there is no missing persons report in the police files—at least none we can find so far."

"You know, Paul," said Jack after a thoughtful pause. "I doubt there ever was one. I remember speaking to Abe's second cousin around that time. We figured he was likely on the skids somewhere—Madison or Milwaukee maybe. The drinking had reached a point, he was killing himself. The one family member I dealt with really didn't know the man and wanted nothing to do with a drunk. Also, I think that Abe had run up enough debt that they wanted to keep their distance from any fall-out that could cost them."

"Do you remember a break-in at the Bobcat Inn?"

"Now that you mention it, I do. Tell you why I remember—Abe called me that day to say he'd be late paying on the medical bills from his wife's death. He had all his receipts from Friday night fish fry in the cash register that night. He never did pay me."

"So maybe that's about the time he disappeared?"

"Could be. Sure enough, the more I think about it. I never had another meal out there either. I would bet you anything that you'll find a tax record a few years later that assumes he passed away. Not missing. Just presumed deceased. That doesn't help much. He must have had lawyer who might know. Maybe check with the town clerk and see if you can locate the estate notice after his wife's death? He would have needed a lawyer for that."

"Thanks, Jack."

Off the phone, Osborne shared Jack's comments with Lew. "Well, let's call it a night, Doc," she said, heaving a sigh. "I'll give you a call after I finish my gardening tomorrow."

———•———

His phone rang at six a.m. the next morning. It was Lew. Osborne leaned up on his pillow. "You're up early. Got the garden all set?"

"I wish. Sorry if I woke you, but I just had a call from Roger. He worked the night shift and he's reporting on two more break-ins that occurred during the night—both times the thieves cut through the roofs with an ax and a handsaw. They hit Bob's Firestone and Family Video.

"A woman walking her dog saw two men leave the back door of Family Video and get into an old convertible they had parked across the street in the Loon Lake Market parking lot. This was three a.m. Not a lot of cars in the parking lot. She called it in about five minutes later, which was too late—but you know what I'm thinking? Somebody's back in town and we should have a little talk."

"Bobby Schradtke owns an old Ford Sunliner—sort of an orange-red color."

"That fits. The woman thought it was reddish-brown, but it was too dark for her to be sure. Just strikes me that those break-ins years ago stopped right around the time he was sent up the river. And a little too coincidental that he happened to be working for one of the places that got robbed. Given his arrest record, I'm dropping in on Mr. Schradtke this morning."

"No gardening?"

"Later. This Schradtke connection is bugging me."

"Lew, you need a day off. Can't it wait until Monday?"

"One hour in town isn't much. I need to determine if I've got probable cause for getting a search warrant."

"Just one thing, Lew—under no circumstances do you cancel our evening."

"I hear you. I promise."

Osborne shook his head as he hung up. He'd believe it when he saw her.

.

CHAPTER 23

"You don't look happy," said Osborne as he opened the driver's side door to help Lew climb out of her truck. "But you do look great. Love the outfit."

"Thought you'd like it," she said with a rueful grin. She was wearing the new khaki fishing shorts and fly fishing shirt he had given her for her birthday. He liked the shirt in particular. Tucked in so it enhanced the curve of her breasts, the shirt had a way of reminding him of pleasant evenings, past and future.

"A disappointing day," Lew said. "But maybe seeing you and spending a little time on the water will improve my mood."

"I promise you it will and now—if you'll grab your fly rod, I'll get your gear and we'll head down to the dock," said Osborne. "I have the canoe ready with a few surprises inside."

As they rounded the house towards the walk down to the water, Osborne noticed her face had fallen. "Lew, what has you so down? Too much time around Mr. Schradtke?"

"Quite the contrary. He wasn't at his mother's, which is where he is supposed to be living. She didn't know where he might be and, in fact, had not seen him since he left yesterday afternoon with his brother, Ron, and a friend of theirs. 'Off to drown a worm' is what they told their mother. You believe that?"

"No sign of his car I take it?"

"Nope. Nothing. No basis on which to get a search warrant to search his mother's house. That's for sure. Kind of a dead end."

"Has he violated his parole by not being there?"

"Tough call. I asked his mother to call me when he shows up. We'll see. The woman definitely shows signs of dementia. Then Ray called. They located the boat that hit C.J.'s jet ski. It had been abandoned two lakes up the chain—pulled up on shore near an empty cabin. I've got Todd checking it for prints but I doubt we'll find much. Ray said it looked like whoever it was wiped it down before leaving it.

"He stopped by the resort that owns the boat. Because it's their ski boat, they keep it full of gas and ready for use on these summer afternoons. Their ski instructor was on his lunch hour when it was stolen. Some kids who were swimming said they saw a pickup drive down to the dock and drop off the guy who took it."

"Can they identify him?" asked Osborne.

"Ray wasn't sure. They're little kids—six year olds. Not the best eyewitnesses, but then the worst witness is the *eye*witness anyway. Haven't I learned that the hard way."

"Well, sweetheart," said Osborne, slinging one arm across her shoulders as they walked down to the canoe that was tied to the dock, "are we ready to set work aside and enjoy the evening?" He held the canoe steady for her to climb in.

Seconds later, they were gliding over the water. The frustration clouding Lew's features gave way as she scanned the surface for signs of feeding insects. These were the moments Osborne loved to watch—the dark beauty of her eyes, the excitement she radiated as she rigged up her fly rod and puzzled over the absolute correct dry fly that might entice a trusting bluegill.

"I thought we'd go up a new 'secret passage' this evening," he said, using the phrase his daughters had coined to name the small, lovely streams that fed into Loon Lake from the surrounding wetlands. "I've never taken you up this one stream that runs down from the northwest. For once, the water is high enough for us to scoot through the culvert that runs under Dragon Fly Road. Good cold water up there."

"You're in charge, Doc," said Lew, resting her paddle across the bow of the canoe as he paddled. The evening was still. Only a hint of a breeze—more like breath on a pane of glass. A great pink sun was beginning its descent in the west. "I love the colors in the sky right now," she said, her voice relaxed and soft. "Lavender and mauve."

"Mauve?" said Osborne.

"Mauve—I had an aunt, my mother's sister, who was an English teacher, and that was one of her favorite words. She wrote poetry."

A shriek from somewhere ahead pierced the calm. Lew straightened up. Osborne stopped paddling. "Sounds like a great horned owl just scored a rabbit," said Osborne.

"Listen," said Lew. "Hear the splashing?" As she spoke two kayakers paddling furiously came into view. A man and a woman whom Osborne guessed to be in their forties. They wore swimming suits and baseball caps and appeared to be out for an evening of leisurely kayaking—except for the terror on both their faces.

"Excuse me," said the man in the front kayak. "Do either of you have a cell phone? We have to call the police."

"I *am* the police," said Lew, "Lewellyn Ferris—I'm with the Loon Lake Police Department. What's wrong?"

"We found part of a dead body," said the man, taking off his baseball cap and wiping sweat from his forehead. "My wife did. She looked in this pail back there. It's awful—"

"Back where? How far back?" said Osborne.

"Back not too far, around a couple bends," said the wife. "Just … a head. I mean the thing in the pail is a human head." She choked as if trying hard not to throw up.

"Wait here for us, will you, please?" asked Lew. "No, wait, why don't you paddle out onto the lake, and about halfway down the shoreline you'll see a light pine shed close to the water. Dr. Osborne's dock is to the left of that. Please paddle down there and wait for us."

"The door off the deck is open if you need anything," said Osborne, "and the dog in the yard is friendly."

"And, please, don't call anyone until we return," said Lew. "We don't need everyone glued to their police scanners crowding into Dr. Osborne's driveway."

---

Two bends later, they came upon an ancient railroad trestle over which ran a snowmobile trail. Hanging off a large nail hammered into one of the wooden supports was a beat-up metal minnow bucket with its lid tipped to one side.

Osborne edged the canoe close to the minnow bucket and Lew got up onto her knees to peer in. "Oh …" she said and backed away fast. "Doc, your turn."

Staring down, Osborne wondered if Bobby Schradtke's eyes were colder in death than in life. He doubted it.

CHAPTER 24

Not even the rocking chair squeaked as Edna Schradtke sat hunched and silent with her eyes closed. A slight shake of the rosary beads clutched in one gnarled hand was the only movement. Osborne and Lew sat on the sofa to her right, waiting.

Finally she tipped her head slightly to the right and said, "Chief Ferris ... tell me how it happened. Was he beaten? You know," she took a deep breath, "his father beat him as a boy. Is that how he died?"

"We don't know," said Lew, answering the question for the third time. She remained patient. "I have officers at the scene gathering what evidence we can find, and when we know, I'll tell you. Right now, it is critical that we find your other son, Ron. As far as we know, the two of you are the last people to have seen Bobby.

"Ron may be able to help us find out who killed your son— or he may be in danger himself. Please try to remember if they mentioned where they were going, who they were with ..."

The old woman rocked slightly in her chair. "People don't understand Bobby. I'm leaving him the house, you know." She opened her eyes and gazed around the room. "He'll be happy here."

"Edna," said Osborne, getting to his feet and walking over to place a hand on her shoulder, "do you have other family members we can call to help you out this evening? You need someone here. Now. We can't leave you like this."

"For heaven sakes, why?" she said. "No family. My brother died last year. But I'm fine. The boys will be home any minute. They take care of me just fine."

"Who lives next door, Edna?" asked Osborne, realizing the woman's short-term memory was hopeless. Likely the shock of hearing of Bobby's death didn't help, even though Lew deliberately withheld the details. "Do you know your neighbors?"

"Of course, I know my neighbors. June Fisher is a dear friend. You know, she lost her husband just a few months ago."

Lew motioned to Osborne and left the living room. He heard the front door close, followed by a murmur of voices. He waited as Edna rocked back and forth, humming. Then he heard the sound of the door opening, and Lew walked back into the room along with a tiny, older woman in a light green bathrobe, her white hair in pink curlers.

"Mrs. Schradtke," said Lew, "June is here to help you out. Maybe you should stay at her place tonight?"

"I heard the sad news about Bobby, hon," said the neighbor, bending over Edna. She glanced up at Lew and Osborne. "Edna's short term memory has been a problem for quite a while, Chief Ferris. We keep an eye on her whenever Ron is gone. I'll see what we can do for her this evening."

"She said you lost your husband recently?" said Osborne, wondering if this small person in her bathrobe had the strength to help Edna who was at least a foot taller.

"No, not me. Luther is fine. I'm sure the shock of the news has Edna even more confused."

"We're trying to find out where her son, Ron, might be," said Lew. "We think he is the last person to have seen his older brother. Do you have any idea where he goes? Is he always gone for days at a time?"

"Heavens, no, he's the one who really takes care of his mother. But it *is* Saturday night. Maybe he's out with Kenny? They work together, play cribbage at Kenny's place some nights."

"And who is Kenny?" said Lew.

"Ron's pal, Kenny Reinka. Lives out by the cemetery. Raises sled dogs."

———·•·———

Leaving Edna's house, Osborne reached for his cell phone to call the one person who knew everyone—and their personal business—in Loon Lake. "Ray, you know a man by the name of Kenny Reinka?"

"Kenny Reinka? Sure do. Quiet fella. Real short. Why?"

"Where's he live?"

"Up behind the old cemetery at the end of Fawn Road. Why?"

"Just a minute," Osborne lowered the cellphone: "Lew, Fawn Road—down at the end.

"Okay," Osborne said to Ray, "but I just have a minute. Here's the situation …" After giving a quick rundown, he listened to a question, then said, "No idea. Severing the head like that—the loss of blood is so severe I don't have the expertise to make any kind of guess as to how long ago it would have happened, but Lew and I both have reason to think it's been within the last twenty-four hours … yes … Todd Martin is at the site where we found Bobby—or that part of him anyway," he added.

"He's securing the area and the route in so forensics can work it in the morning. Lew has a call in to Wausau but she could use your help, too."

"Of course, but—"

"Not a word to anyone until we know more."

Lew tapped Osborne on the arm, "Ask him to drive out to Curt Calverson's—check on the place, see if Calverson's home, ask him if he's seen or heard anything unusual. But call ahead and let him know he's coming."

"I heard that, Doc. I'm on my way. Watch out for Kenny's dogs—those are big puppies he's got."

With Lew at the wheel, the Loon Lake police cruiser sped down Lincoln Street, over the new bypass and onto the county road leading to Kenny Reinka's place. No lights, no siren.

Osborne threw a quick glance into the back seat, making sure his 20-gauge was secured by the seat belt. It was.

It was midnight when they started up the rutted drive in front of the small house. A clear sky and the glow of a high, bright moon outlined the two-story house perched at the top of a slow rise. A series of five small huts lined the drive all the way up to the house and beside each one Osborne could make out the dark, hulking shapes of huskies hunkered down in the warm night air. He hoped they were chained.

"Open your door slow, Lew," he said, "I'm worried about those dogs."

"We're not stopping here," said Lew, swinging the steering wheel to the left as she drove up onto the grass. She had switched on the cruiser's searchlight and its beam picked up a car backed into the woods off to the left of the rear of the house.

"That's Bobby's car!" said Osborne, sitting forward. The top was down, making it easy to see the trunk was open. Lew stopped about fifty yards from the car just as a man in a light-colored t-shirt and jeans ran from the woods towards them.

"Stop right there," shouted Lew as she got out of the car and crouched behind the open door, her Sig Sauer pointed at the runner.

"Kenny! Get back here!" shouted a heavy voice from the woods. A gunshot sounded, and the man in the t-shirt leapt into the air before twisting and falling.

"Ron Schradtke—come out with your hands up!" shouted Lew. The answer was another gunshot shattering the windshield of the cruiser just as Osborne slid out the passenger side. "Doc? Doc?" shouted Lew.

"I'm okay."

"Stay down!"

One more gunshot from the woods, then the crisp pop of Lew firing her Sig Sauer. Quiet. A long minute … still quiet. No sound from the woods. Lew ducked and ran towards the man in the t-shirt, which was rapidly darkening with blood.

"Can you hear me?" she said as she dropped to her knees.

"He got me in the shoulder," said the man, clutching his upper arm.

"Don't move. We'll get some pressure on that but first I'm calling an ambulance—are you Kenny Reinka?"

"Yes. That's Ron Schradtke in the woods. He's out of his mind. Keep him away from me. Oh, God, there's so much blood …" The man turned his head away and started to sob.

"Take it easy," said Lew, patting him. "You're going to be okay. This is all over." Staying low to the ground and taking care to avoid the beam from the searchlight, Lew edged her way in the direction of the old convertible.

Osborne stayed beside Kenny. He ripped away the t-shirt and wadded it into a pressure bandage, which he held against the wound to staunch the bleeding until the paramedics could take over.

———•———

After handing Kenny off to the first of two paramedics arriving with the ambulance, he headed over to where Lew stood staring into the trunk of the Ford Sunliner. Alongside the rear tires were mounds of fresh dirt. What remained of Bobby Schradtke lay curled in the trunk of his car.

"And then there is this," said Lew with a wave of her hand towards the half-dug grave. Bobby's younger sibling—wider, heavier, darker than his big brother—lay with his head and shoulders in the pit he'd intended for Bobby. Ron Schradtke wouldn't be finishing that job: Lew's bullet had entered above the right eye, killing him instantly.

"Hard end to a long evening, Doc."

"Oh ..," said Osborne. He shook his head, "I feel sorry for Edna."

"I don't know that I can agree with you. She protected Bobby. You have to wonder why."

CHAPTER 25

The hospital corridor was bustling as if it were a Monday, not a Sunday. "Oh, it's always like this on Sundays," said a young nurse at the look of amazement on Osborne's face. Lew and Osborne paused at the door to Kenny Reinka's room. The door stood open halfway. Even though the nurses' station had told them it was okay to enter, they peered around just to be sure.

Kenny was sitting up in bed, the bandage on his right shoulder visible under the pale blue hospital gown, his color much better than it had been when they had last seen him at two that morning.

"Kenny, the doctor said you're feeling well enough to talk—is that right? You okay sitting up for a while?" asked Lew in a brisk tone. She had her notepad out and was already pulling out a chair as Kenny gave a weak smile.

Under wispy strands of light brown hair, Kenny's face was round and worn, toasted orange brown by too many seasons in the sun. His eyes were small and round, too—their pupils pinpoints of black against the blue of his irises. In spite of the bony, slender frame visible under the thin coverlet, he reminded Osborne of a pumpkin with a half smile carved into it.

It was a smile of hesitation wed to worry—certainly not pleasure—at the sight of the Chief of the Loon Lake Police Department and her deputy. It was a thin-lipped smile that telegraphed, "oh shit, what happens next and how bad will it be?"

"Kenny, I'd like Dr. Osborne to sit in on our conversation. He assists the department with forensics and I've got some questions along that line—"

"That's fine," said Kenny, shifting slightly against his pillow. "I know Doc. You put my plate in a while back," he said, looking at Osborne. "Remember? My dogs took off with the sled and I ended up face down on that stump?" To demonstrate, Kenny pulled the fixed plate from his mouth, waved it in the air and put it back in.

"Sure, folks. Ask away. Sorry I was in such bad shape last night. Feel a lot less shaky today. You saved my life, Chief. Ron was out of his mind crazy. I couldn't believe it when he showed up at my place, at first. I thought he was making a joke when he asked would I help him bury Bobby.

"Once I knew he was serious—when I saw what he had in the trunk of the car—I kept trying to get away and call for help but he wouldn't let me out of his sight. Wouldn't even let me feed the dogs. He was foxy weird. I didn't know what he'd do next, and I was scared. Man, was I scared. No way have I ever known Ron to be like that. Wild. All over the place screaming how Bobby cheated him out of his life, his mother, his home—everything. And you know what … he wasn't even drinking."

"What set him off do you think?"

"I don't think—I *know*. Bit of a story 'cause it starts way back if you ask me," said Kenny, grasping the rails on his hospital bed with his good arm and pulling himself up a little higher up on his pillow. "Here, need help?" said Osborne getting up from his chair to boost Kenny's good side.

"Thanks, Doc." Kenny took a long sip through the straw in his jug of ice water, then said, "I've known Ron since first grade and I can tell you that even though Bobby was a teenager when we were little kids, he picked on Ron. Bad stuff, too. Burned him with cigarettes, knocked him around …" Kenny rolled his eyes and said, "Worse, even—if you know what I mean …"

Lew raised her pen from her notepad but not her eyes, "Molested maybe?"

"You know there were two girls in that family, too. Both dead now. Y'know, I don't know who was worse: Bobby or their old man. But I tell 'ya that after the old man fell out of his fishing boat and drowned—I think Bobby was around fourteen when that happened … After he died it was like Bobby became the man of the family—in an evil way. Y'know? Just *evil*. He for sure did stuff to his sisters.

"Ron knew about it, maybe even saw it. Never said anything happened to him, but I tell you he could get real dark when he was drinking. When the demons came out, I made it my business to leave, get out of his way."

"How much do you drink, Kenny?" said Lew.

"Oh, I'll have a brewski now and then. Two's my limit. Feel too bad in the morning if I have more. I decided years ago to feel good every morning." Kenny managed a grin.

"Smoke dope?"

"Nah, can't afford the stuff. Nothing like that for me. Put my money in my dogs, dumb as that must sound."

"Not at all. So Ron was a heavy drinker?"

"Off and on. Any talk about Bobby was only when he was really drunk and some goofball at the bar might bring up the old stories. You know—Bobby's burglaries, stealing cars, beating up the shop teacher at the high school, that stuff. One guy said he'd heard Bobby had stashed a pile of cash somewhere—asked Ron if that was true.

"One thing I'll never forget happened to Ron when we were still kids, maybe fifth grade. Late one winter night he showed up at my folks' place with all these welts on his back and no clothes on except his underpants—said he tried to tell his mother that Bobby did it but she didn't believe him. He ran away he was so scared. My mom put First Aid cream on him and he slept at our house that night.

"Bobby still pulls shit on Ron. I seen him kick his brother for no reason. He's always chewing on a toothpick and more'n once I seen him spit the damn things into Ron's food. Little stuff, but mean. Just plain mean.

"On the other hand, Bobby protected him, too. From other kids. You know how kids like to beat each other up when they're twelve, fifteen? Bobby kept 'em all scared to death so no one touched Ron. Guess you could say Ron had a love-hate thing with his big brother.

"In fact that's what was going on this week. Right when Bobby got back to town was the same day that Ron and I get screwed over by this Calverson guy we done some logging for. We told Bobby about it and he got all excited about pay-back. Said he picked up some new ideas while up the river."

"You mean, go after Calverson?" said Lew.

"I mean he was going to rough the guy up 'til he paid us, but when he found out the guy owns the bank where Mrs. Schradtke keeps her money and the bank won't let her have it—it got worse. It was one thing that Calverson owed Ron and me, but their old lady? *That* Bobby did not like—not one bit."

"You're saying it was Curt Calverson who owed you and Ron money?" asked Osborne. "What for? How much?"

"Oh, shit, he owed us each twenty-five hundred bucks— we worked hard as hell logging that back forty for him. The day we go to get paid, the sonofabitch stares us down and re-fuses to pay. Said he knew we were on unemployment all winter so he didn't have to pay up."

"Ah," said Lew, "so that's what spurred Bobby to go to bat for Ron—is that it?"

"That and the old lady's missing bank account."

"Did that just happen? The bank account, I mean."

"No, I think it's been going on. But it was right when Bobby got home from the slammer that one of the neighbor ladies who had been helping Mrs. Schradtke with her gov-ernment forms happened to stop by. She's the one told the boys that Edna's government benefit payments were way down because of some loan she had with Calverson Finance.

"Bobby got real cold when he heard that. I can tell you right now that ever since I was a kid and first knew the guy—when he goes cold, you get out of his way. He doesn't care if you're male or female or a little kid. He's gonna smack somebody. That's when I told Ron I didn't know what they were up to, but I wanted no part of it.

"But he kept talking to me. He was getting more and more excited, see. That's when those two started hanging out in the woods back behind the Calverson's lake place. They wanted money and they wanted to hurt the guy."

"Did you know Bobby stole a boat and rammed Calverson's wife on her jet ski?" Lew asked.

"They thought it was her husband on it. Ron said they were watching from across the lake with binoculars. See, we knew from working out there that Calverson always took either his jet ski or his pontoon out in the afternoons when it was nice. We knew his habits—like when he would go to town to get his mail, that kind of stuff."

"Go back to Ron and Bobby for a minute," said Lew. "If they were operating together to try to get back at Curt Calverson, what set Ron off against Bobby?"

"Oh, yeah, he told me all about it when he drove up with Bobby in the trunk. Two things happened yesterday. First, Edna had one of her anger spells and went after Ron. You know how her memory has been going? Well, she sometimes has these rages—her eyes get like Bobby's when she's so crazy mad. Usually Ron could settle her down but this time she ranted that she was leaving the house to Bobby. She started throwing stuff at Ron and Bobby thought it was funny. He egged her on.

"The other thing went wrong was ..." Consternation cramped Kenny's face as if he realized he had just said too much.

"Keep going," said Lew. "Another thing went wrong ..."

"Okay ... I learned something from Ron when he got to my place last night that I swear I didn't know before." Kenny looked worried as he spoke. "Chief Ferris, you gotta believe me when I tell you this."

"Kenny, I'll do my best."

"You're gonna think I'm an accomplice or something ..."

"Let me decide that. Tell me what it is, and we'll see."

"Bobby and Ron have been robbing a couple places lately. According to Ron, Bobby has this surefire way of getting into bars and stores from the roof that can't be traced."

"Right," said Lew, "we just had someone rob Family Video by cutting a hole in the roof."

"That was Bobby—and Ron. What happened was after they left the video store where they got a nice bundle of cash, Bobby told Ron he wasn't gonna give him half like he promised he would. Ron said they stole over three thousand bucks but Bobby said all he'd give Ron was a couple hundred. A couple hundred? That did it for Ron.

"Add it all up—he's losing the house to Bobby, Bobby's taking over their mother's money. Ron only makes a few thousand a year. Living with his mother is all he has besides that truck of his. Hell, he doesn't even have a dog. The guy cracked. I wonder he didn't kill his brother a long time ago."

"Well, he finally did," said Lew, "and mutilated the body."

"Yeah … I saw that," said Kenny, raising his eyebrows as if he still couldn't believe it.

"We're hoping you might have some idea where all this took place, Kenny," said Osborne.

"I know where he shot him, all right. Ron said he got himself calmed down after that set-to with his mother and Bobby and invited Bobby out to see his deer stand." Kenny was quiet for a moment. "Used Bobby's own chain saw on him. Smiled when he said it, too. I'll bet you'll find the chain saw back by that deer stand."

"Do I assume the deer stand is further back along that snowmobile trail that runs over the railroad trestle where the bucket was hanging?" asked Lew.

"Yep. 'Bout a mile in. That's paper mill land. They let anyone who wants hunt there. Ron's had that deer stand for years. So he put Bobby's head in a pail? Weird, huh? You know," said Kenny, comfortable now, "Ron was right about one thing. If he could've got Bobby buried, who was going to worry about the guy? I mean, other than their mother, and she might forget he was even home. Who would care?"

"Kenny, does the name Abe Conjurski mean anything to you?"

"Sure. His wife was a friend of my mom's. They ran the Bobcat Inn, right? My folks and I ate there lots. Why?"

"Bobby worked there for awhile," said Lew. "Did he ever mention that?"

"My mom sure did, and I kinda remember the story. It was right after Mrs. Conjurski died and Abe was having a hard time. He was trying to run the restaurant but the help kept quitting because of his drinking. He got the county jail to let him hire some of the work release guys and Bobby was one of 'em, so that's how come he was washing dishes there. One night the gal who was waiting tables accused Bobby of stealing her tips. He had been clearing tables so she figured it had to be him.

"Mr. Conjurski kept an eye out and he saw Bobby slip some tips into his pocket. Confronted him right away. But he was good about it. He told Bobby if he returned the money, he could keep his job. My folks thought that was a mistake."

"Sounds like Abe to keep him on," said Osborne. "He was a nice man."

"I think it was because he had enough problems already. He couldn't afford to lose a dishwasher. Then he got robbed—course it was Bobby who robbed him."

"How do you know that?"

"Hell, Bobby bragged about it. Thing about Bobby—couldn't keep his mouth shut." Kenny laughed a dry laugh. "Bragged about everything. Said he made sure Abe would never turn him in, too."

Kenny looked up at the ceiling. "Now all that was a while ago and you can bet your ass I didn't ask any questions. Put it this way: when Bobby talked I tried not to listen. Guy was dangerous. Just being around Bobby Schradtke could creep you out."

"Kenny," said Lew, setting her pen down and looking at the injured man, "this brings me back to why Ron would have severed his brother's head. Why put it in a minnow bucket? Has Ron always been that nuts?"

Kenny's good hand twisted the blanket. "Some things you don't forget from when you were a kid, and maybe this means something. When Ron and I were in second grade and made our First Communion, Ron's grandmother gave him a kitten. A real cute little kitty—all black with these tiny white paws. He loved that little guy. Named him 'Rambo.' One day we come home from school, stop by Ron's house and there's his kitten in the front yard … with his head chopped off. Bobby done it."

"Last question," said Lew, "why did Ron shoot at *you*? You're his best friend."

"I dunno—except maybe he was losing me, too? I wanted out of there, man."

CHAPTER 26

L ew put down the phone, leaned back against her chair and gazed across her desk at Osborne, who had just walked in. "Not a bad start to the week, Doc. That was Bruce Peters. They found a toothpick stuck in the rug holding Abe Conjurski's remains. Since we sent Bobby's remains down to Wausau along with the chain saw to confirm that's what was used on him, they have plenty to work with to see if they can match the DNA from the toothpick to Bobby."

"Any news on how he might have killed poor Abe?"

"Still working on it. Summer holidays, they're a little backed up down there. Could be a few weeks until we have all the details."

"My other call was from the FBI agent who is dropping by Curt Calverson's this morning. Have you heard how C.J. is doing? I'm worried about her. She's about to get some bad news on that husband of hers. They froze his assets, they have a search warrant for both their houses, and they shut down his Illinois office over the weekend."

"Guess that explains why Curt was so slow to open the door when you sent Ray out to check on him Saturday night—think he was expecting the FBI?"

"Might have been. He should have greeted Ray with open arms. Given the rampage Ron Schradtke was on, he's lucky to be alive. Instead, it's poor C.J. who got the worst of it."

"I have a status report on C.J. Ray stopped by my place late last night after he had been in to see her. She regained consciousness yesterday morning and the swelling is going down. Her doctors are optimistic she can be released before the end of the week. Ray's over there with her right now."

"I know we have a fishing date with a certain young lady at ten this morning, Doc," said Lew with a wink, "but let's drop by the hospital first and see when would be a good time to talk to C.J. I don't want her blindsided."

———⊷∘⊷———

"Guess who's sitting up," said Ray, meeting Lew and Osborne outside C.J.'s room. "I just dropped by to let C.J. know Nick's team made the semi-finals in the tournament. If she'll get better fast, I promised I'd take her to watch the finals on the Fourth."

"She's doing that well?" Osborne was surprised.

"C.J.," said Ray, opening the door, "are you up to more company? Chief Ferris and Doc are here."

"Sure, if they don't mind a girl with two black eyes." Her voice sounded strong.

"Really," said Lew, stepping into the hospital room behind Ray. "We don't want to tire you out."

"Oh, don't worry," said C.J. If it hadn't been for the brave, sweet smile she managed as they walked in, Osborne would have thought he was meeting a human raccoon: two black eyes and a band of dark purple bruising across the forehead masked C.J.'s face. "And I already heard about Curt, so you aren't going to upset me," she said.

"How did that happen?" asked Lew, "I told the agents that you were in serious condition and not to approach you—"

"They didn't. My mom called from Chicago because she heard it on the news. I have to say I'm not surprised—I knew he was up to something. Always very secretive, and he would never tell me anything about his business."

She looked over at Osborne and Lew, who had seated themselves in the chairs at the end of her bed. "I know you must wonder why I married Curt—the age difference and ..."

"Only if you feel like talking about it," said Lew, "we all have our reasons for doing things others don't understand."

"I don't mind, really. He was a client of mine at the fitness center I ran in Evanston. He was single, well-to-do and—I know you won't believe this—he courted me. He was so attentive and gave me lots of gifts. But right after we married—boom! It was over. He stopped talking to me, looked annoyed when I spoke up. I felt like I was his secretary or driver or ... or ... "

"So maybe what's happening isn't all bad," said Osborne.

"Not at all," said C.J. "A relief—gives me a good reason to move on."

"The bad news is that they're arresting your husband on a variety of charges including bank fraud and bribery of state officials. I'm afraid they are freezing all his assets. You won't have access to any bank accounts, the homes."

C.J. smiled. "I'm going to be okay, Chief Ferris. That was all dirty money anyway. Who wants it?"

"But what will you do?"

"My folks will tide me over for a few months. I'll open another fitness center. I'm a big girl."

"You can't do that until you've finished your casting lessons," said Osborne.

"Oh, hey, Nick and I have plans for you," said Ray. "Do you need a place to stay? I've got an extra bedroom. Might have a job for you, too. I got that audition for *Ice Men* next week? Nick's going to help me with equipment but I sure could use a woman's eye to help me look good—"

"Ray," laughed C.J., "let me recover and then we'll talk. Okay?" She looked around the room at the three people gathered there. "With friends like you," she said, her eyes on Ray, "I'm not worried about things. Right now, I just want to be beautiful again."

"But you *are* beautiful," said Ray, kissing her on the forehead.

"Doc," Lew thrust a thumb towards the door, "time to go. We've got a date, remember?"

CHAPTER 27

"So, Mason," said Lew as she watched Mason thread a night crawler onto her hook. "Your grandfather and I wanted you to see all the new fencing that was put up to keep people off the island."

"Yeah," said Mason as she cast her line into the shallow waters of the Kiddie Fishpond.

"We found out who that boy was who scared you. Right after you told your grandfather about him, Officer Roger was able to catch him scaring some other children. I talked to his parents and I don't think he'll be bothering anyone here again."

"Yeah," said Mason. She nodded but kept her eyes on her bobber.

"Sweetie, Chief Ferris and I want you to feel safe here," said Osborne, putting his hand on Mason's shoulder.

She looked up at him, "I do, Grandpa."

"But, honey," said Lew, placing a hand on her other shoulder, "we want to keep everyone safe and the only way we can do that is for you to tell us if you see something you think isn't right. Don't hesitate. And if you are worried someone might hurt you for doing that—just call 911 or the police—and tell them what you see. You don't even have to tell them your name. So promise me you will be a brave girl and do that next time?

"Yeah," said Mason. This time she met Lew's eyes with a shy smile. "I promise. Oh! Oh! Oh! I have a bite!"

———

"Thank you, Lewellyn," said Osborne after they dropped Mason off at her house—with a string of four nice crappies, "you gave her a way to protect herself. I didn't know a person can call the police like that—report something happening and not give your name."

"Happens all the time, Doc. Just last week we had a call from a worried mother. An older kid on the block was frightening her children with a deer rifle. Other parents in the neighborhood refused to report it out of fear of the family who owned the gun. The father has been arrested for domestic abuse. All we needed was the call. She didn't have to identify herself and we were able to get a dangerous situation under control.

———

"Lewellyn," said Osborne, whispering in Lew's ear as she lay beside him later that night, "Thursday is the Fourth of July—think you can take the day off?" Her face was luminous in the moonlight. She smiled.

"Maybe. What do you have in mind?"

"How 'bout those bluegills that are still waiting for us?"

"I'd rather not go up that same creek for a while. Crime scenes are like ex-husbands—I prefer to avoid them."

"Sorry. Forget the bluegills, let's take some streamers and go after muskies. I know," Osborne's voice rose with excitement, "I'll show you my secret muskie hole up on the Pelican River. Not even Ray knows it.

"Oh, and you know what else? I was looking in my fly boxes the other day and I have this Yellow Striped Marabou Pike Deceiver that Erin's kids gave me for Father's Day. That might be perfect in this weather for muskies. Size four, six inches long—"

"Doc? Doc."

"What?"

"Do you always talk fishing when you have a woman in your bed with no clothes on?"

He laughed. The dog barked and then she did that thing she always does—and he surrendered.

**Victoria Houston** fishes and writes in northern Wisconsin. Along with her critically acclaimed Loon Lake mystery series, she has written several non-fiction titles. Visit www.victoriahouston.com for more information.